FINDING HARMONY

The Sydney Roberts Series–Book One

Susan Hart Snyder

Cover design by Micah Kearns
Author photo by Patti Sewall

Finding Harmony/ Susan Hart Snyder -- 2nd Ed.
ISBN-13: 78-0-9974224-1-2
LCCN: 2015903505

To my mother, sweet Dixie, who brings harmony into the lives of everyone who shares her world.

Life is either a daring adventure or nothing. To keep our faces toward change and behave like free spirits in the presence of fate is strength undefeatable.

Helen Keller

CHAPTER ONE

Kicking a tumbleweed the size of a Volkswagen beetle aside, I cupped my hand over my eyes to block the intense afternoon sun and searched the road in both directions for any sign of life. Two days into my self-imposed journey of discovery and I didn't have a clue where I was. I was soon to discover, however, that it was not the Promised Land.

It had been such a dramatic departure too ... epic. Selling off most of my worldly goods, I packed up my Basset Hound and black and white cat, said a tearful but resolute good-bye to my ex. Hopping into my–well, not exactly *my*–motorhome, I set my compass for New York. It was time to forge a new life for my faithful companions and myself.

There I was, stranded on what must be the least traveled road in America, with no idea why the blue whale of the vehicle kingdom would sputter, clank, and refuse to go another mile. The motorhome was not my ideal choice of a medium from which to divine a new life, but it had given me the impetus to do so.

When I received the news that my part of my Uncle George's estate was his beloved motorhome, I was touched by the thought, but far from thrilled by the gift. My cousin Ralph, who had come out for the memorial service from New York, offered to trade me a few months in his basement apartment in the Bronx for it. By then I had already made up my mind to move from L.A., and the Northeast seemed like a good choice–plenty of culture and a lot of opportunity for work as an editor.

The only catch was that I would have to deliver the motorhome to Ralph. He couldn't miss any more work. I had always wanted to do the *Travels with Charlie* thing, so why not?

Day one had gone great, too–L.A. to Vegas without a hitch–unless you consider the few tree branches I took out while learning to maneuver down side streets. Mr. Bumbles, that's my sad-eyed hound, and Alice, my saggy-bellied cat, and I thoroughly enjoyed our first evening cozied up in a casino parking lot under the neon glow of the Strip.

Day two had also begun well, with the three of us humming north on Interstate 15, and enjoying the air conditioning fan ruffling my hair, Alice's fur, and Mr. Bumbles' ears. It would have been much more poetic if the wind had been doing the ruffling, but late August is not exactly a window down time of the year in the Nevada desert.

Midday was spent at a quaint little park in St. George, Utah, after a short stop at a local supermarket where I added to my already well-stocked larder. When he glanced through the motorhome's cupboards, Harry, my ex, suggested that I had laid in enough food to supply a small scout troop for a year. But you can never have too many Fritos, *really*, even Alice likes them.

The source of my current predicament can be traced to that park in St. George, for it was there I met a little man with a very little Chihuahua, who insisted I take a detour to Zion National Park. He assured me that it would not be far out of my way, that there would be plenty of other people at the campground, and that its beauty would take my breath away. All I had to do was follow the scenic route out of town and I would be there in less than an hour.

Two hours later, the dust filling my lungs took my breath away all right. After one more glance in each direction, I decided help was not coming to find me, so I was going to have to find it.

Stepping back into the motorhome, I hooked Mr. Bumbles' leash to his collar and cast a glance at Alice, who was curled up in the driver's seat. She tends to take advantage of any opportunity to show who's really in charge. I debated whether to take her along, but decided it was impossible. There was no way that cat was going to stay in my arms for a minute, let alone all the way to the row of buildings I had noticed in the distance quite a ways back.

After cracking two windows, grabbing my purse and water, then locking all the doors, Mr. Bumbles and I headed out along the red silt strip next to the road. We had gone quite a distance, but progress was slow due to Mr. Bumbles' proclivity for inspecting every bush and anointing it with his personal holy water. Suddenly, he made a low woof, yanked on the leash, and took off after a cottontail rabbit that we scared up.

There was absolutely no way Mr. B was going to catch that thing, but his hound nose told him otherwise, and at sixty-five pounds, when the dog makes up his mind, there's no changing it. My only choice was to hang on until his legs or desire gave out. And hang on I did, until my right foot came into contact with a particularly low shrub and I took an ungainly swan dive into the dirt.

Before lifting my head, I did a mental damage assessment. Judging from the way my hands and knees were burning, they were obviously well scraped, and I was pretty sure the warm trickle down my left leg must be blood. I had a piercing pain in my right ankle, and as I ran my tongue around my mouth I realized that one of those bits of grit that I tasted was actually a tiny chunk of my left front tooth.

Moaning, I carefully rolled over and sat up. Yep, my shin was definitely bleeding, my ankle was definitely sprained, my tooth was definitely chipped, and I was definitely in deep shit.

Swiveling my head, I spied my purse a few feet away, the contents scattered. I noticed that the water bottle was missing just about the same time I felt a lump under my left rear cheek—one of the two I'm always promising to trim and tighten—in my dreams. Dragging the split plastic container out, I watched in morbid fascination as the last drop of water plopped to the red earth, leaving a nice little crimson puddle. Jeez, could things get any worse?

My hopes lifted as I noticed my cellphone sticking out from under a nearby bush. Dragging it toward me with my good left heel, I grabbed it, turned it on and held my breath as I waited for an indication that I was within range of a cell. Nope. No service. God knows why I thought the signal would be any better there than back at the motorhome. Useless piece of shit! I started to launch my phone to the heavens, then thought the better of it. After all, I wasn't going to be stuck in that little corner of Hell forever.

Or, was I?

Scanning the horizon, I began to worry about Mr. Bumbles. He had been gone for several minutes and I could no longer hear his baying. My only hope was that his loyalty and his nose would guide him back to me. In any event, I couldn't just sit there and wait for him. I was already very thirsty and I had no desire to spend the night with whatever critters lurked nearby. I prefer to keep the spooky monsters of the animal kingdom at a safe distance behind the glass of my television set.

Standing up, I tried putting a little weight on my bad ankle. Not so good, but it had to do. Moving slowly, I gathered up my belongings and was doing a slow 360 when I spotted the outline of the buildings that we had passed. They were still pretty far away, but if I continued across the desert in the direction that Mr. Bumbles had dragged me, it would certainly be a lot shorter than retracing my route back out to the road and the motorhome.

After what seemed like hours, but by my watch was thirty minutes, I was standing on a decomposed granite path leading to one of what looked like several dormitory buildings positioned in a regimentally straight row. The thing was, though, there was no evidence of a college in the immediate area, there was a very high chain-link fence around each building, and a very nasty looking dog roped to a cottonwood tree in this particular yard. I was pretty sure it wasn't a prison, but the whole place definitely had that narrow-windowed, cement-block jail motif–definitely not *Home and Garden Television* material.

I decided that rather than face the dog I would take my chances on the next dorm down. Had I seen myself in a mirror, I may have been able to attribute some of the treatment I received from the inhabitants of the strange enclave to sheer fright of the wild figure hobbling down their walk, in blood-streaked clothing and with auburn hair whipped into a *Bride of Frankenstein* frenzy.

As I approached the next gate, I noticed they too had a dog roped to a cottonwood. Mr. Bumbles. What a relief. When he saw me, he did the Bumbles happy dance, which involves much tail wagging, two full circles, and a series of low woofs. By the time he finished, his legs were hopelessly entangled in the rope, and without thinking I lifted the latch, pushed through the gate, and gimped over to him.

"Hey, boy" I stroked his dusty head. "Am I ever glad to see you."

Bending over and balancing on my good foot, I was untangling the rope when I noticed a flicker out of the corner of my eye. As I looked up, a flash of pink fabric disappeared around the corner of the building. I opened my mouth to call out, but my words were cut short by a deep male voice booming down on top of me, "You're trespassing!"

The little stability I was relying on to support me while helping Mr. B completely faltered as my heart rocketed to my throat and my shoulders jumped to my ears. I made my second unplanned dive of the day into Utah dirt, landing on my side, my bad ankle thrust in the air and pointing directly at a glowering face.

"Jesus, you frightened me. I didn't see you," I blurted out, the pulse in my ears so loud I felt like I was standing next to Niagara Falls.

"You *will not* take the Lord's name in vain!" The wrinkles between his world record length eyebrows drew into cavernous depths. "Now, get up!"

"Oh, uh, sorry." With shaking hands, I shifted my weight to my bottom, then reached down and cradled my ankle. "It's sprained." I lamely stared at his worn boots, afraid to look up. Mr. Bumbles had moved over next to me, so close the drops from his overhanging tongue were landing in my lap, but I didn't push him away. I needed somebody on my side.

Several seconds ticked off as the man continued to loom over me, apparently waiting for me to get up, which was just not going to happen, at least not without support. "I can't stand on it." I nodded my head at my ankle then finally dragged my eyes up to meet his chin. Making contact with his eyes was still asking a bit too much for my nerves.

Reaching down, he roughly pulled me to my feet and quickly drew back. Waving my arms like a tightrope walker, I finally regained a bit of my balance. When I finally found the courage to look over at him, he was not nearly as tall as he had seemed from my recumbent position. At five feet eleven, I am generally at or higher than eye level with many of the men I meet, and he was no exception. His lack of height, however, didn't do anything to detract from his menacing stance. With bulging crossed forearms and a head far too large for his body, he reminded me of Popeye with a Brutus attitude.

"Why are you here?" he asked never taking his eyes off my face.

"My motorhome broke down and no cars came by, so I remembered seeing your buildings and was heading this direction." My nervousness shifted my speech into high gear.

"My dog took off after a rabbit. I tripped and sprained my ankle, then the dog got away. I spotted him here tied to your tree, so I let myself in," I finished, finally allowing myself to breathe.

"That's your dog?" he asked, staring at Mr. Bumbles.

"Yes." It came out more like a sigh.

"Angela!"

Whoa! There he went with the shouting again, and just when my heartbeat was beginning to slow down.

"Angela! I know you're back there. Get over here right now!"

I followed his gaze to the corner of the building where I thought I had seen movement. A thin, blonde-haired girl of about six slowly sidled around the building, head down.

"Hurry up!" he snapped.

She moved more quickly, but never raised her head. When she came within reach, he clamped his hand on her shoulder and drew her to stand directly in front of him.

"Where did this dog come from?" he asked.

"I found it," she murmured to the ground.

"Look at me when I talk to you," he snapped, lifting her chin with his index finger.

"I found it," she repeated softly, eyes glistening.

"Where?"

"The yard."

"Is that your answer?" He squeezed her chin.

After several moments, she closed her eyes and shook her head from side to side.

"Where, then?"

"Behind the house." She lifted her featherweight arm and pointed. "I thought he was lost."

"And does Mother Helen know you went out of the yard to get him?"

A trace of fear crossed her face then faded as she shook her head again.

"Then you need to march in the house and tell her what you have done."

"Yes, Father." The inflection and tempo of her words indicated they had been well practiced, but her eyes reflected more resignation than respect.

Turning her around by her shoulders, he gave her a soft shove in the direction of the large front door.

"Thanks for finding Mr. Bumbles for me," I called after her.

Glancing back over her shoulder, she mouthed the words, Mr. Bumbles, but didn't look at me or acknowledge what I had said.

"You have to leave." Mr. Congeniality untied the rope from Mr. Bumbles' leash and started to wind it around his hand.

"And exactly how do you expect me to do that?"

"That's really not my concern, now is it." He tucked the last of the rope into his palm and made a fist.

I stared at his balled hand. What was he planning to do, knock me out? "Look at me, Mister." I threw my arms out and teetered precariously on my good foot. "I'm not going anywhere without some help."

With blazing eyes, he surveyed me from head to foot then stared off into the distance, obviously trying to decide what to do. Finally, he grouched, "Wait here," and strode toward the door.

I looked down at Mr. Bumbles, who had been patiently watching the scene from his favorite position–seated, then bent over and picked up the end of his leash. "This is one fine mess we've gotten ourselves into, boy." I ran my thumb over the knot on the top of his head. He commiserated by raising an eyebrow.

After several minutes of staring at the front door, trying to determine if I had been abandoned, it finally opened and a woman who looked like the poster child for *Prairie Home Companion* walked down the steps carrying a white plastic chair. As she came closer I realized I had highly overestimated her age. She couldn't have been more than fifteen. Fifteen? And very pregnant. Is this a home for unwed mothers, I wondered, looking past her at the gray facade? Do they even have those anymore? But then, what about Mr. Congeniality and the little girl? None of it was adding up.

Averting her eyes, she set the chair down next to me. She lost her struggle with her curiosity, however, as she stole a peek at me under her dark lashes. Her face immediately reddened when I caught her eye, and she started to rush off, her long brown braid thumping her back. "Wait, please," I called after her. "I need ice for my ankle, and some water." The desperation in my voice must have been convincing because she stopped and turned around. "I'm totally dehydrated and Mr. Bumbles is too."

"Mr. Bumbles?" She frowned.

"My dog." I nodded at him.

"Oh." The beginning of a smile crept into her eyes and mouth as she looked at him, but quickly vanished.

"Please?"

"All right." She disappeared back into the house.

I guided myself into the chair, placing my right leg straight out in front of me. Mr. Bumbles plopped down beside me. After a few minutes, my Nightingale in calico returned with a plastic bag of ice and a cup of water for me, and a stainless steel bowl of water for Mr. B. Again, she turned to hurry off after making her delivery, but I gently placed my fingers on her forearm.

Stiffening like a plaster cast, she hesitated. I seized the moment. "Please don't rush away." I lightly pressed my fingers into her arm. "I really need to know what's going on."

"What do you mean?" She jerked her arm away from my hand, her voice a mixture of suspicion and fear.

My radar was buzzing big time. What the hell kind of place is this? Resisting the urge to shout that very question to the sky, knowing that she'd bolt, I calmly explained, "I need to know if your father is going to help me."

"Husband."

The cup of water was halfway to my lips when her answer sunk in. I dropped the cup back down. The water could wait. "Husband." It was a statement, not a question.

"Yes."

Scanning her face, I tried to assess her feelings about mothering the child of a man I estimated to be at least three times her age, but it revealed nothing. I was impressed. She had trained herself well.

"Well then, do you happen to know if your *husband* is going to help me?" I allowed myself two long draws of water as I waited for her answer.

"I am sure that he will. He is a benevolent man."

"That's comforting. He sounds like a real treasure," I said, far more sarcastically than I had intended. Her eyes widened. I quickly changed the subject. "What's your name?"

She set her jaw as if she was willing herself not to speak, and finally said, "Ruthie."

"Ruthie. Very pretty. I'm Sydney." I extended my hand, but she made no move to take it. Instead she looked over at the house.

"I have to help with dinner."

"Okay, Ruthie." I gave up, sensing that keeping her there was going to be next to impossible anyway. "You go. Thanks for the water and ice, and best wishes on that baby." I lifted my cup in a mock toast.

Her face reddened, much deeper this time. "Oh." She instinctively set her hand on her tight round belly. "Thanks."

"You might throw a little water our way if we're still sitting here in the morning." I smiled.

The beginnings of her own smile appeared again, but this time only reached as far as her eyes before another female voice called sharply from the door, "Ruthie!" like a mother to the fifteen-year-old child that she was. I was only able to catch a glimpse of a long brown and silver braid as the two of them faded into the dusk of the house.

I had just managed to figure out the best way to keep ice on my ankle when Mr. Congeniality was back towering over me.

"I called the town mechanic. He'll be here after he closes his shop." He put his hand on the back of my chair, brushing my shoulder.

Startled, I leaned forward, wondering what he was doing.

"You can wait on the road beyond the gate." He tipped the chair forward, barely giving me a chance to remove the ice from my ankle and get my feet set.

"That's really generous of you." Clenching my jaw, I adjusted my purse over my shoulder and held Mr. Bumble's leash in one hand and the ice in the other.

Mr. Congeniality's response was to march deliberately to the gate, unlatch it, walk fifty paces down the road, set the chair down, and return just in time to pass me as I was hobbling slowly through the gate like an octogenarian on a field trip.

"Benevolent," I said to the air as I heard him shut the door to the house behind me.

CHAPTER TWO

I looked at my watch again–two hours. *Two hours.* Mr. Bumbles and I had shared the last of the melted ice thirty minutes before, and I was so parched my tongue was permanently affixed to the roof of my mouth. I was now lying on the dirt with my throbbing ankle propped on the seat of the chair, far beyond caring what might be crawling through my hair.

There were two good pieces of news, however. One was that neither Mr. B nor I had any inclination to pee, something that both of us do quite often, but something I would have been far from inclined to do out here in front of God, Mr. Congeniality, and company. I mention the latter, for in my growing hallucinatory state I imagined that he and all the members of his merry little band were watching us from an upstairs window.

The second cheery thought was that it was August, and even though the afternoon had melted into evening, it was still quite light outside–light enough for me to see the buzzards as they swooped down to rip the flesh from my bones!

Dropping my foot from the chair, I made myself sit up. Studying the road again, I focused on the high flat-topped mountains in the distance. Who would live in a place like this? Swiveling my head around to take in the abodes behind me, I answered my own question, and gave them the one finger salute just in case my hallucination turned out to be correct.

My imagination had just moved on to compiling a list of ways to repay the hospitality of my *hosts* when I heard the rumbling of a very loud engine headed my way. Bouncing along, kicking up dust, was a rusty military truck that looked like it should have been mothballed after the Korean War. Through the cracked windshield, I could just make out the top of a dark head. As the truck rolled to a stop, I noticed three mottled blue-black dogs, with faces remarkably similar to Mr. B's, yapping in the back. I couldn't hear them over the engine and was thankful that Mr. Bumbles hadn't seen them, because it gave me a chance to grab his leash.

A toothpick flew out the driver's door, followed by a man of medium height and slight build wearing orange coveralls–the kind that they distribute at the state penitentiary. Great. I looked over at the house. First Mr. Congeniality, now a prison escapee. What is it with the men in this area? Will the people in the house hear me if I scream? They probably wouldn't come anyway.

"You the lady with the motorhome?" he asked.

"Yes," I croaked out between parched lips.

"Calvin Wheatly." He slapped one unlaced canvas camouflage boot down in front of the other until he had crossed way too far into my personal space. Quite the ensemble he had going.

I took a small step back. "Sydney Roberts," I mumbled.

He inched a little closer. "Man, you don't look so good." He tilted his head slightly as he stared at my face, then dropped his chin to look at my ankle.

"I fell." I shrugged my shoulders.

"I'll say." His gray eyes bored into my face again. "You crack your tooth?"

"Among other things."

"That musta been some fall." Squatting down, he turned his attention to Mr. Bumbles. "Hey, boy." He ran his hand over Bumbles' back while Mr. B whipped his tail back and forth in response. "Nice hound. You hunt?"

"Nooo." I wondered if the guy had just shown up to chat. "Look, could we get to the motorhome," I said curtly, then instantly regretted it. The last thing I wanted to do was make the guy mad. Orange jumpsuit notwithstanding, he was the only hope I'd had in hours.

"Sure, lady." He stood up. "Where's it at?" He looked around.

"Down the road a couple miles."

"You walk all this way on a bad ankle?" He frowned at my foot.

"I thought someone in one of those houses might be able to help me." I tilted my head toward them. "But, they only gave me a little water and ice and called you."

He clicked his tongue and shook his head. "They don't like to be bothered."

"That's the understatement of the year. Who are those people, anyway?"

"Polygamists," he answered as nonplussed as if he had just declared them to be Methodists.

"Polygamists?" My eyebrows shot up to my hairline as I thought over my brief encounter with them. Well, duh. How dense could I be?

"Warren Jeffs. You probably heard a' him. He was from these parts. Ended up down in Texas. That's where the law finally caught up with him. Rottin' away in prison now. But, there's still plenty a' other groups of 'em in the US and Canada, Mexico even. They purty much keep to themselves so as to escape notice."

"Except for the ones on reality TV looking for their fifteen minutes of fame."

"Huh?"

"You know, those reality shows about polygamists?"

"Nah. My TV broked a while back. Don't miss it." Taking Mr. Bumble's leash, he guided me by my elbow to the truck. At least he was a polite ex-con. "Where you hail from, anyway?" he asked, helping Mr. Bumbles into the cab of the truck.

"Los Angeles."

"Had you figured for a Californian." Climbing onto the seat, he stretched out his arm toward me. "Give me your hand, put your good foot on the runner, and I'll pull you up." He grabbed my hand. "You can tell the Californians by their tans. Folks around here spend a lot more time looking for shade than sun."

I glanced down at my white freckled skin and wondered exactly how he was interpreting that as a tan.

As we approached the motorhome, it became clear that another vehicle had finally shown up while I was on my little jaunt, for Uncle George's pride and joy was now covered in shocking pink and apple green graffiti, wheels to roof, bumper to bumper. Bracing my hands on the dash, I sucked in my breath. Entirely oblivious to my body language, Calvin gave me a suspicious glance. "You one a' those Greenpeace protesters?" he asked.

"Of course not!" I scowled at him.

"You don't have to get so defensive. It was only a question." He squeaked the truck to a stop.

Unsuccessfully trying to squash the rising panic in my chest and reminding myself again that good 'ol prison-suited Calvin was my only hope, I offered a quick, "Sorry," and grabbed for the door handle. Jerking it up and down with all my might, I could not get the damn thing to open. One final jerk and the handle came off in my hand. Dangling it between my thumb and index finger, I held it out to Calvin.

"You gotta calm down, woman." He plucked it from me and laid it on the dash. "No need to get violent." Methodically opening his own door and stepping down from the cab, he reached up and lifted Mr. B down, then put his hand out for me.

Red faced, I apologized yet again to Calvin as I slid across the seat and he helped me to the ground. Hobbling over to the motorhome as quickly as I could, my first thought was of Alice. What if the sicko taggers had gotten inside? My worst fears were realized when I saw that the side door had been pried open and was hanging by one hinge.

"Alice! Here kitty, kitty, kitty!" I screeched, so loudly that even if Alice were still there, she would probably run in the opposite direction. "Alice, where are you?" I forced my voice into a high singsong pitch as I stepped into the motorhome, scanned the cab and kitchen area then headed for the small bedroom in the rear.

"Alice," I let out a deep sigh for there she was balled up on my pillow. "Are you all right?" I stroked her fur and attempted to turn her on her back to check her out. She repaid my concern by folding her paws around my hand, claws at the ready. "Well, you obviously survived the ordeal intact. I might have known."

Turning my attention to the bedroom itself, I noticed that two of the built-in drawers were half open. Scanning the contents of those and the other two drawers and closets, I didn't see anything missing. They were just my clothes after all, probably far too conservative for the average tagger. Then my eyes fell on the shelf over the bed. "Damn it! They swiped the Dodger cap and Sandy Koufax bobblehead doll that Uncle George willed to me with the motorhome!"

"Looks like they helped themselves to your pantry too." Calvin filled the tiny opening to the bedroom. "You better come take a look."

A quick inventory reflected their junk food palettes, for the missing items included the six-pack of diet root beers in the fridge, and every bag of Fritos, cereal, and cookies in the cupboard. The bagged salads were, of course, left intact.

"That just absolutely does it!" I plopped down on the dinette seat, then popped right back up, my heart racing. Flipping the cushion up, I lifted the lid to the storage area underneath and pulled out a banker's box and a softbound computer case. Nothing had been touched. "Thank God!" I exhaled, and quickly put the lid back on the box. "My work," was all I offered as an explanation when I realized Calvin was watching me.

"We best get movin' with figurin' out what's wrong with this vehicle. It's startin' to get dark." Calvin nodded toward the open door.

I followed him outside. While he was checking the motor, I made a full circle of the RV, trying to make some sense of the graffiti. It was glaringly obvious that my taggers were the single biggest dimwits in Utah. Anything over four letters was invariably misspelled, a likely reason for more than a dozen *Fuck* this or thats, and an equal number of *Shits. Anarky Rules!* was a particular favorite for managing to be both misspelled and an oxymoron. I gave them a six out of ten for effort on that one. And who uses pink and green to tag, anyway? "Morons!" I rubbed my finger over one of the *Shits*. It was stuck good.

"Looks like a rusted gas tank and bad fuel line." Calvin came around the corner of the motorhome with Mr. Bumbles at his heals, wiping his hands on a faded red rag. Mr. B seemed to really like the guy.

"How long will it take to fix it?"

"You don't fix a gas tank. You replace it."

"Well then, how long will it take to replace it?"

"Depends." He scratched the back of his head.

"On what, exactly?" What was this, Twenty Questions?

"On how long it takes me to track one down."

"So, what's your best guess as to how long all that will take?"

"I can't rightly say." He looked over at the motorhome. "What year is the thing?"

"I don't know." My voice again took on the edge Calvin didn't like. I breathed deeply. "I think my Uncle George bought it sometime in the nineties."

He pondered that for what seemed like five minutes, drawing a toothpick out of his shirt pocket. "Fer now, I'll tow her to the garage, and start tryin' to track down a gas tank and fuel line in the morning." He slid the toothpick between his molars.

"Okay." I could live with that. It was the best news I'd heard in hours.

"You're sure it's safe here?" Standing in the doorway of the motorhome, I peered through the dark at the outline of the cars and parts in varying states of decay that surrounded us.

"Ma'am, this is Harmony, Utah, population seventeen-hundred and thirty-five, includin' the outlying areas and the livestock, the majority of 'em asleep by now. Nothin' happens here." He turned and started to head to the garage.

"They can't all be harmless. Look at this motorhome." I nervously fingered the broken latch on the door, wondering how I was going to lock myself in for the night.

"Bored teenagers." He looked back over his shoulder. "The dogs'll chase off any intruders or critters, and I'll be within shoutin' distance just up there." He pointed to a window above the garage then raised his hand to signal good-bye.

"Oh, that makes me feel a lot better," I said under my breath.

Deciding that I could use some company, I called loudly into the dark for Mr. Bumbles. He trotted up accompanied by Calvin's dogs, which were, according to their owner, prizewinning coonhounds. Coonhounds? I almost laughed out loud. So, where was Elmer Fudd? But, he was serious. Turns out he was a hunter of the bigger game variety–elk, bear–figured.

"Come on, Bumbles." I patted my leg, but he just stood there panting and staring up at me with this sort of sophomoric, *Ah gee, can't I just hang with the guys*, look on his face. "Oh, all right, go on you." I motioned them away. I didn't want to deny Mr. B a reunion with his long-lost cousins.

Dragging Grandad's rocker out from where I had it wedged between the bed and wall, I inched it past the kitchen area and set it in front of the door. Like that was somehow going to impede an intruder. Grandad's rocker was the one impractical item I was not willing to give up when I sold off the rest of my furniture. Too many memories of him sitting in it, poring over his finger-worn photo albums and telling stories of his early days in Los Angeles to anyone within earshot, regardless of how many times they'd heard the tale before.

Family gossip was that Grandad took a lot of poetic license with his yarns, but hyperbolic or not, those stories of a Southern California sparsely populated and ripe with the smell of orange and gardenia blossoms and filled with opportunity were one of the driving forces behind my desire to find my own utopia.

But, shit, I lowered myself onto the worn oak seat and raised my right leg onto the dinette cushion, what had I gotten myself into? I was so ill-equipped to deal with this type of venture it was pathetic. I thought about calling Harry. Wouldn't that just make his night to discover that less than forty-eight hours after my departure his prediction that I'd never make it was correct?

Nope. I wouldn't give him the satisfaction. I was on my own.

I was suddenly so tired I thought I'd better get up before I fell asleep right in the rocker. Walking into the mini bathroom, which was definitely not designed for not-so-mini me, I caught a glimpse of myself in the mirror–frightening! What I wouldn't give for a long hot shower, but that wasn't going to happen. The water pressure in Uncle Harry's motorhome amounted to a trickle. Definitely not enough to make it through my Medusa mop to my scalp.

I raised my arm and pointed my nose in that direction. Whoa! I quickly squished my arm to my side. Was I ever ripe! I would have to find someplace to shower first thing in the morning, or even Calvin wouldn't want to get within ten feet of me.

CHAPTER THREE

As I walked away from the garage, I slipped my sunglasses on, hoping they would somehow help hide my mess of a body, kind of like the trapped rabbit that believes if it sits really still, the fox won't notice it. Dumb. At least I had managed to mask my gamy odor through a sponge bath and lots of powder, and although my ankle was still a bit swollen, I could actually put some weight on it. My hair and tooth were another story. Wiry red hair takes massive amounts of water and an arsenal of product to control, that or braids and a baseball cap, size extra-large. I was forced to resort to the latter.

A trip to the local dentist was the first item on a to-do-list that included the sheriff's office to file a report on my taggers, and some kind of facility where I could shower. Calvin had offered to let me use his, but I wasn't that desperate–yet. When I asked about a motel, he said that the only one in town had closed down a few years ago on account of they don't get many tourists. No kidding. It was one pitiful little place. I headed in the direction that Calvin said would lead to the dentist's office.

The concept of a city planning department had apparently not reached Harmony, Utah, for the buildings were laid out like a well-shuffled deck of cards. Calvin's garage, for instance, was set between a private home and a laundromat. The section I was currently passing looked like Main Street after a Saharan sandstorm, with cracked sidewalks, tattered awnings, and an inch-thick coating of silt on the window frames. Its businesses included a small market, a bank, and a diner with a painted sign over the door labeled *Dusty's.* Appropriate. Judging from the number of trucks parked nose in to the brick facade it was the local hangout. I hurried by it as quickly as my gimpy ankle would allow, as there was a synchronized head turn in my direction when I passed the restaurant windows.

Just about the time I thought I was going to run out of town, I reached a faded yellow clapboard house with a green lettered sign out front that read *V.A. Loomis, D.D.S.* As I pulled on the screen door handle to let myself in, the hinges screeched in such a high nails-on-the-chalkboard pitch that the hairs on the back of my neck stood on end. I let go of it like it was made of molten lava. It slammed against its frame and my neck hairs reached record height.

Several seconds later, I was still standing on the wrong side of the door deliberating on how to open it without jeopardizing my hearing when it was pushed open from the inside, accompanied again by that teeth-vibrating screech.

"Shouldn't somebody fix that thing?" I asked of the silhouette that had stepped aside to let me in. Realizing that the interior was far too dark for sunglasses, I removed them and waited a few seconds for my eyes to adjust. When the room came into focus, I discovered that drawn shades and thrift store lamps with low-wattage bulbs were the source of the dusky atmosphere in a room that was far more akin to 1950's parlor than medical office.

"That's how V.A. knows someone's here."

"Huh?" I had momentarily forgotten about my doorman. Turning to face him, I was really sorry I had removed my sunglass disguise, for standing before me was the Marlboro Man. I mean it. If they were still hawking cigarettes on the tube this guy would have the part. In fact, I had a hard time believing the wardrobe department at Paramount Studios hadn't dressed him. From sun-crinkled piercing blue eyes to worn leather tooled boots, he was quintessential cowboy.

"She uses it instead of a doorbell." He nodded toward the door.

"Oh." I acted like I understood, but I really didn't. Lowering my cap on my forehead and pretending to scratch my lip to cover my chipped tooth, I asked, "Is there a receptionist?"

"No. Just V.A." He took a seat at one end of a careworn chenille couch, and picked up the book that was on the end table next to him, opened it, set aside a crocheted bookmark, and began to read.

"V.A.?" I was still standing in the middle of the room.

"Yeah, V.A. Loomis. She's the dentist." He put his index finger on a line of the book and looked up at me. His look indicated either annoyance or curiosity, I couldn't tell which.

"I saw the sign." I shifted under his gaze, really sorry I hadn't looked for the shower *before* the dentist. "I just hadn't paid particular attention. Kind of unusual for a woman to use initials instead of her name."

"I suppose." He dropped his eyes back to his book. Not a real chatty fellow.

"So, do you think that she'll be out any time soon?" I stood rooted to my spot on the floor, unsure whether to stay or come back later.

"Should be," he answered, not bothering to take his nose out of the book.

"Okay, then." I moved over to a vinyl padded kitchen chair under the front window and took a seat. Several minutes passed by in which I exhausted my patience for sitting with absolutely nothing to do. There were magazines on the end table next to Marlboro Man, but that would mean crossing over in front of him, and I wasn't too sure that my sponge bath and powder were holding.

I had decided to resort to my fallback activity of sorting through the items in my shoulder bag, and was just setting it on my lap, when a loud low moan carried through the inner office door. I looked over at my silent companion to see if he had heard it, but he just kept right on reading. Shrugging my shoulders, I started to unzip my bag when the moaning struck up again, this time much louder. What on earth kind of Marquise de Sade dentist is she? I wondered. Running my tongue over my chipped tooth, I decided I could live with it until I reached New York. I could probably even file the rough edges myself.

I zipped my bag and started to stand, but sat back down when the inner door opened and the mournful wailing began moving toward a crescendo. I froze in place when out walked a short, sunbaked man struggling under the weight of a huge tan dog that was completely limp except for its mouth, which was working overtime. The man's straw cowboy hat had been knocked to the side and was barely clinging to his head. Following him through the door was a woman almost a head taller than him, with shoulders that would make a linebacker envious. A lab coat identified her as the dentist, or at least some sort of medical professional.

"Just take him home and let him sleep it off," she was yelling to the man over the wailing, "and be sure to give him the full course of the meds. We don't want any infection." She crossed the room and opened the screen door, so screeching now accompanied the moaning. Then she straightened the man's hat on his head as he passed under her, and let the door slam shut as the final note in the symphony from Hell.

"Funny how some dogs will do that under sedation," she chuckled more to herself than us. Then to the man, "Just let me straighten the examination room, and I'll be right with you, Noah."

"Sure, V.A. I have some to go in this chapter anyway." He tapped his book. "How far along are you?"

"Done. Finished it last night. It's going to be a good one for discussion, don't you think?"

"Oh, yeah. Amazing how relevant it still is."

Okay, I looked from one to the other. The place had moved way beyond the strange and was heading perilously close to the absurd. New York was sounding better all the time.

My heart sank as V.A. glanced over at me. My opportunity to slip away unnoticed had passed. She walked over and stopped only a foot from my chair, making it feel like she was towering over me. "And what can I do for you, Missy?" she asked.

Missy? Oh boy, the last person to call me that and get away with it was my junior high school gym teacher, but I suppose I was going to let this one slide, given she had the appearance of someone you just didn't want to cross. "Uh, well," I cleared my throat, "I'm a little confused. I thought this gentleman here said you were a dentist, but the dog..." I held my hand out in the direction of the screen door.

"Ha!" Her laugh blasted over me like a foghorn. "I can see why you might be confused. I'm just filling in for Hank Zimmerman, the vet, while he's out to Oklahoma City with his daughter at a horse show."

"You're a veterinarian also?" I asked.

"Nah. Just a lot of time with animals and, of course, the dentistry helps."

"Okay," I said tentatively.

"Now, what's it that you need?"

"Well." I hesitated, wondering if I really wanted this woman working on my mouth after the beast that was just carried out the door had slobbered on her.

I guess my indecision was transparent, because her tone did a one eighty. "I don't have a lot of time, hon." She put a fist to her hip. "If you're queasy about my work, you might want to head over to St. George, because in Harmony I'm it." She started to turn away.

My face flushed. Damn. I managed to make her mad anyway. That mousy part of me that can't stand being disliked stopped her. "Oh, wait, sorry. I, uh, I chipped my tooth." I lamely pointed to it and looked over at Marlboro Man, who had been identified as Noah. I guess his book wasn't as interesting as he said, because he had been watching the exchange and now had a half smile on his face I interpreted as a smirk. I scowled at him and his smirk turned into a broad grin.

And I thought cowboys were supposed to be the kindly type. This one definitely had a mean streak.

"Well, just have a seat then, and I'll see you after Noah here." V.A. disappeared through the office door.

An hour later, I was stretched out in the dentist's chair with my mouth full of V.A.'s large but surprisingly gentle fingers. She had been firing bullets of information at me nonstop from the time I sat down. The topics ranged from international politics to the price of hay per bale, about which she seemed equally well informed.

"There you go, Missy." She pulled back to admire her handiwork. "All done for now." She patted my cheek, the last gesture I would ever expect from my L.A. dentist. But then this wasn't L.A. "You're going to need to have that thing bonded unless you like the character it adds to your smile. Ha!" She blasted another laugh at me.

"My red hair and height give me all the character I can handle, thank you very much." I slipped my legs over the side of the chair, stood, and looked at V.A., instantly regretting the height remark. "Uh. It feels a lot smoother." I ran my tongue over my tooth, changing the subject.

"Good." She let the remark pass. "Let's go check the books and see when we can get you in to finish the job."

"Oh. I'm only here for a short time while Calvin Wheatly fixes my motorhome. I'll have it bonded when I get to New York." I followed her down the hall and through the door to the reception area.

"Cal, huh?" She looked back at me over her shoulder. "What's wrong with the motorhome?"

"A rusted gas tank," I said slowly, not thrilled with the way she said *Cal*.

"You might want to count on it taking more than a short while." She picked up an appointment book on the desk in the outer office and started thumbing through it.

"Why is that?" I asked, my voice raising an octave with the beginnings of panic.

"Well, hon, Cal's a very good mechanic, but he likes to take his time."

"But, I don't have a lot of time. I need to get to New York." I slung my bag over my shoulder. "Perhaps you can recommend another mechanic."

"There is no other mechanic in town." She flattened the book open on the desk. "Let's see. I have an opening day after tomorrow at ten."

Was the woman listening? I wasn't going to be hanging around this dump of a town for that long. "Perhaps I should check with Cal first."

"You do that, Missy, but in the meantime, I'll just pencil you in." She made a note in her book, closed it, and started walking me to the door.

Anxious to finish my errands and get back to Cal so I could ask him just how long the repair job was going to take, I hurriedly pulled on the screen door handle. The accompanying screech jerked my forward momentum to a halt and V.A. bumped into me, making me embarrassingly aware once again of how I must look and more importantly smell. I wondered how she had tolerated bending over me to work on my tooth. After I stepped over the threshold to put some distance between us, I turned back and asked, "Do you know of a campground or any kind of exercise facility around here that has a shower?"

"Ha!" Her trumpet laugh heralded the ridiculousness of my question and I felt my face grow hot. "In case you haven't noticed, this isn't exactly a vacation destination." She gestured toward the poor excuse for a town center. "And folks around here get all the exercise they need from the source the good Lord intended, hard physical labor."

"Oh sure, that's understandable," I mumbled, starting to turn away.

"But if it's a shower you need, I've got one right here." She nodded toward the interior of the house.

"You do?"

"Yes. We've had indoor plumbing for quite a few years now." Her tone was serious, but she only maintained it for a few seconds before the corners of her mouth turned up and her blue eyes crinkled at the edges.

With very red cheeks, I returned her smile. "I apologize for the question. I was just surprised that you have a shower in your office."

"It's my home, too. And, like I said, you're more than welcome to use the shower."

Since I had no other prospects, I only hesitated a moment before accepting. "When should I come back?"

"I'm booked solid through the afternoon, and since my patients occasionally use the bathroom, you best come back, let's say, right after dinner."

"Thanks. I really appreciate it." I shifted my weight and my bag to my good side and reached for the porch rail.

"I noticed you favoring that ankle." V.A. looked down at my right leg. "You sprain it?"

"I think so. I'm not sure. Do you think I ought to have it checked out? Is there a doctor in town?"

"It doesn't look too bad." She bent over for a closer look. "Nothing a little time off your feet won't cure."

"You're sure I don't need to see a doctor?"

"The only doc we got, Missy, is Norman Schrum, a mostly retired quack, who only sees patients when he's sober, which is the occasional Monday morning. I wouldn't even allow him to treat an ailing rat."

"Okay then," I said, thinking, tell me what you really think. Wow, she was direct.

"You'd be a lot better off just hurrying back to your motorhome, elevating your foot, and putting an ice bag on it."

"And I'll do that as soon as I can, but first I have to talk to someone from law enforcement about your local taggers. They made a mess of my RV."

"The Bailey boys. Good luck on that one."

"You know who they are?"

"Sure. In a town this size the troublemakers stand out like a turd on snow."

She did have a way with words. "But, if you know who they are, why isn't something done about it?"

"They haven't caught them in the act, and those boys are really good at hiding behind their momma's sequined apron strings."

"Huh?" I frowned. Jeez, V.A. was hard to follow.

There was to be no clarification, however, for she was already halfway into the house. "I have to get ready for my next patient, hon."

"But I at least want to report it."

"Deputy Sheriff Crane's office is just behind Dusty's. See you this evening," her voice trailed off as she walked to the back.

As I approached the deputy's office, high-pitched shrieking reverberated through the sun-bleached door, kind of like a flock of harpies had taken up residence inside. I continued on in anyway, determined to finish my appointed rounds, fast becoming hardened to anything I might find in this little piece of the Underworld.

Or so I thought. For as the scene in front of me registered, my jaw dropped so far that one of those harpies could have roosted in my mouth. A platinum blond, forty-something woman wearing a Catholic schoolgirl skirt from Britney Spears' wardrobe–the early years–was leaning so far over the deputy's desk that there was enough flesh flashing from the top of her spiked heeled boots to the T in her thong underwear to please the most lustful of strip club patrons. With her face less than a foot from the deputy's, the inch-long nail on her wagging index finger threatened to slash his cheek clean open.

He had pushed his chair as far back as the wall behind his desk allowed, and in an impressively controlled voice was saying, "Now, Mrs. Bailey, you know that it is my job to investigate crimes committed in this town, and part of that investigation includes interrogating suspects."

"Suspects! Floyd and Lloyd suspects! You have absolutely no evidence it was my boys who broke into Mrs. Anderson's shed! Their lives have been traumatic enough with the death of their daddy without having you haul them in here for no good reason." She turned her head to the left, and I followed her glance over to a long wooden bench on which sat two slumped-shouldered teenage boys completely absorbed in their phones, although how they could see the screens through their long greasy bangs, I don't know.

I started to look back at their mother when three red scratches on the forearm of the boy farthest from me caught my attention. Those streaks looked suspiciously like cat scratches, and I knew just the cat to do it. Taking one step closer to them, I examined their clothing for telltale pink and green paint splotches. There were none there, but these had to be my taggers, the little shits. I glanced over at their mother, who had her eyes locked on me in a *who the hell are you* stare that made me step away from the boys as if *I* was the one who had done something wrong.

Fortunately, the deputy drew the fire back to himself as his patience crumbled around the edges. Taking a few seconds before he spoke, he swallowed, his Adam's apple bobbing just above the stiff collar of his shirt. "Their daddy died thirteen years ago, Mrs. Bailey. They were three. And I had a very good reason to question the boys. Mrs. Anderson said she saw Lloyd and Floyd near her place on several occasions."

"Mrs. Anderson is as blind as a bat, and you know it! And how dare you minimize their grief." She jutted her finger at him once again. How the man could stay so calm with those nails waving across his face, I do not know.

"I want you to stay away from my boys, do you hear me? And as far as your *job* is concerned, don't count on having any kind of job in Harmony ever again!" On that final note, Mrs. Bailey slid her weight back onto her boots, tugged at her skirt, shifted her considerable breasts in her bra, whipped around and ran smack into me. Not missing a beat, she incorporated me into her exit by shoving me aside with her forearm and waggling her fat fanny to the door, where she turned and called, "Boys, let's go."

Apparently not as into high drama as their mother, Floyd and Lloyd spoiled the scene when they required her to shriek, "Boys, let's go!" two more times before they finally dragged themselves off the bench and lumbered along, using the hems of their pant legs to buff the floor as they went.

Following their exit through wire-framed glasses, the deputy half-consciously shuffled a few papers around a desk that looked like it hadn't seen daylight in decades, and looked up at me.

"Wow, you're good." I pulled my bag up higher on my shoulder and moved closer to his desk. "I think I might have had to smack her."

One corner of his mouth turned up, but he was clearly trying to maintain a sense of professionalism. "Not a good plan if I want to keep my job."

"According to Mrs. Bailey, you're not going to have one for very long anyway."

"Mrs. Bailey enjoys throwing her weight around, but there's not a lot behind it."

"Oh, I don't know, I saw quite a bit of *behind* as she was walking out the door."

This time the smile reached his large brown eyes as he laughed out loud.

"Sydney Roberts." I reached my hand across his desk.

"Patrick Crane." Unfolding his tall lanky frame from his chair, he stood and extended his hand to me, maintaining the smile in his eyes. "What may I do for you, Sydney Roberts?"

"Yesterday, my motorhome broke down outside of town, and while I was looking for help someone tagged the entire thing with pink and green paint. Oh, and they also broke in and stole my Dodger cap and Sandy Koufax bobblehead. I'm guessing it was those two stellar young citizens who just left, at least from the scratches I saw on the arm of one of them."

"Scratches?"

"Yeah. My cat was in the motorhome when they broke in, and she's not very tolerant of strangers, or anyone for that matter, me even. So, if they got anywhere near her, I'm sure she let them have it."

"Well, I'm afraid we're going to need more evidence than a cat scratch, but I'll get the details from you and we'll see what we can do. And I won't hold your being a Dodger fan against you." He smiled.

CHAPTER FOUR

Walking up to the motorhome, I noticed Cal swinging the door back and forth to an audience of Mr. Bumbles and his coonhound pals. "All fixed." He slid a screwdriver into his back pocket.

"Really? The whole thing?" I asked, suddenly elated by the thought of putting Harmony, Utah far behind me.

"Just like brand new." He proudly manipulated the lock on the door.

"So, what do I owe you?"

"Nothin' for now. You can pay me when the job's done."

"But, you just said that it *was* done."

He hesitated, giving my comment as much consideration as if I had just read him the Final Jeopardy answer, then he slowly shook his head. "No. I don't believe I said that."

"Yes, you did. You said, just like brand new."

"And she is." He patted the door.

"A brand new door isn't going to get me very far, now is it?" I crossed my arms. "What about the rest of it?" Jeez, this guy could bring out the bitch in me.

Looking as hound-dog hurt as Mr. Bumbles after he's been scolded, Cal shook his head again, and in a maddeningly patient teacher-to-student tone, he said, "Now, miss, I told you yesterday the parts gotta be sent. They couldn't 'a gotten here by today, now could they."

"Okay," I leveled my voice. "When *will* they get here?"

Pulling a toothpick out of his pocket, he twirled it between his fingers. "I couldn't manage to drum up the parts in St. George, so I had to call on up to Salt Lake. They're runnin' a search right now and promised to call as soon as they locate them. Said they should have a bead on them some time tomorrow." He slid the toothpick into his mouth.

"Fine." At least he was offering something tangible. "When they call, tell them I want the parts overnighted."

He pulled the toothpick out. "Gee whiz, you sure you wanna do that? It's gonna cost you a gold mine."

Looking around at Cal's yard sized tossed salad of rusted metal and thinking I didn't want to spend one more night there than I had to, I said, "Oh yeah."

Walking up V.A. Loomis' steps, I had only one thing on my mind, steaming hot water and lots of it, so when a young pregnant woman stepped around the screechy screen door holding her hand to her face, it took me a few seconds to realize it was Ruthie, wife number *God knows what* of Mr. Congeniality. From her shocked expression, she was not expecting to run into me again either.

"Ruthie," I said, as I closed the gap between us. "Hello. How are you?"

"Okay." She continued to hold her hand to her face while glancing over her shoulder through the screen door.

"Do you have a bad tooth?"

"Yes." She patted her jaw. "Doctor Loomis says that pregnant women sometimes end up with problem teeth. I probably need a root canal, but we decided against it because I shouldn't be taking a lot of painkillers."

"It must hurt a lot." I lightly touched my hand to her forearm. I couldn't help it. I take full responsibility for being a patter. It's kind of my religion. A wave of pain crossed her face, and I moved my hand to her shoulder. "Here," I gestured to the porch swing, "why don't you sit a minute."

Before we took our first step, Ruthie's *husband* shoved his way through the screen, knocked my hand off her shoulder, grabbed Ruthie tightly by the upper arm and started pulling her down the steps.

My anger flared like a roman candle. "Stop that! You're hurting her!" I rushed after them. His reaction was to pull her even harder to his truck, which was parked in front. "What is the matter with you? Stop it, now!" I was so close he had to feel my breath on his neck.

Snapping his head around to face me, he growled, "Leave us be!"

"No. I'm not going to leave you *be*. You're abusing your pregnant wife, you bastard."

Letting Ruthie go so that he could turn fully around and square his powerful shoulders up with my puny ones, he silently unleashed the full force of his fury on me entirely through his eyes. Creepy. The color drained from my face and fear supplanted my anger, but I held my ground, fully expecting him to deck me a good one. My eyes wide open, I studied his as he fought an internal battle with control.

Finally, he bent so close I could smell what he'd had for lunch *and* breakfast, then he rasped, "Don't ever go near her again."

Backing up a step, the blood rushing in my ears, I mustered a wavering last word. "I will stay away, but I will also be filing a report with the deputy sheriff regarding your abusive behavior."

His reaction to my warning was even scarier than his physical threat, for he started to laugh, a mean ugly laugh. "You do that, lady, you just do that." He opened the passenger door and pushed Ruthie in. Then he walked around to the driver's side, hopped in, revved his engine, and took off. Ruthie sat facing forward, ramrod straight.

"My God, did you see the way he treated her?" I asked V.A. when I encountered her standing on the porch, obviously having witnessed the whole scene. My heart was still beating hard against my chest. "He's an animal! He needs to be locked up."

"And you want to be the one to do it?" V.A. pulled on the noisy screen door and moved aside to let me in.

"No." I stepped over the threshold. "God, no."

"The way you went after him says otherwise." V.A. stared hard at me then walked to the reception desk and closed her appointment book.

"Well, somebody needs to do something about him, don't you think? I can't imagine people just standing by and letting him get away with basically raping a minor and pushing her around. Cal told me that the guy is a polygamist. Isn't that against the law?"

"It's complicated. They've been fighting over the laws regarding plural marriage for over a hundred years in this state. Those who practice it keep to themselves and usually avoid the attention of the authorities, unless they wander into territory like fraud and money laundering."

"So, if a polygamist defrauds the government, the feds step in. But, if he marries a girl three times younger than himself, they leave him alone? That sure sounds criminal to me!"

"Some folks don't see it that way."

Was that a defensive tone in V.A.'s voice? I wondered, as I watched her concentrate on tidying the things on her desk. It didn't make any sense that someone who appeared to be as no nonsense as V.A. would be comfortable with defending a lifestyle that tolerated abuse. "What's the creep's name, anyway?" I asked.

"Samuel Vaullie."

"I take it you think it would do no good for me to report his actions to Deputy Crane."

"Never said that." V.A. moved the chair out from behind the desk and placed it next to the couch.

"So then I should."

"That's entirely up to you, Missy." V.A. pulled the two chrome kitchen chairs from under the window to form a half circle with the couch.

There she went with the Missy again. What was it about that nickname that raised my hackles? "Then I think I will do just that, first thing in the morning. I'll just add another name to my ever-expanding list of thugs who seem to make a practice of getting away with whatever they like around here."

Oops. I must have gone too far with that accusation. V.A. stopped rearranging furniture and gave me a long hard stare. I quickly changed the subject before she had a chance to respond. "Are you having company?" I asked.

"Book club." She pulled one of the pillows off the couch and began to fluff it up.

"Of course. I heard you mention it earlier."

"Your ankle any better?"

"Yeah, it is. Thanks for asking. The ice did help." I watched her replace the pillows. "Are you sure that it's still okay for me to use your bathroom?"

"Not a problem if you hurry along. There are cleaning supplies under the sink for you to use after you're through."

"Sure." The woman was definitely not shy about delegating. "Is it down the hall here?"

"Last door on the left."

Scrubbing two days' worth of Utah grime from my body was the single most pleasurable physical experience I'd had in months. Pathetic. That I could get so excited about a shower was a sad reflection on my life being seriously devoid of all things carnal for way too long. There was sex with Harry, but that couldn't really even be counted in the carnal category. No. Sex with him was more of the couch potato variety. He'd set down the remote because it was a slow inning or quarter, and grunt, "Hey, you wanna make love." Depending on my mood, he'd either be back to his game right away or fifteen minutes later.

In fairness to Harry, the couch potato thing did have its upside. It was comfortable, like flannel pajamas. And in a place like L.A., which is all bright lights, loud noises and hard edges, flannel can be a good thing. The problem was I had become a prisoner to that comfort. Spontaneity was out of the question when even a shopping trip needed a major battle plan in order to actually find a parking space. And a drive to the beach on a balmy summer evening? Yeah right, just you, your lover, and the million other souls who decided they also wanted a feel of that cool ocean breeze.

My life had become as predictable as a fast food restaurant menu. If I didn't make some changes there was a good chance I'd end up as one of those corpses they find lying in her apartment between stacks of old magazines and newspapers, having her toes nibbled off by one of her forty-three cats. Yuk.

I guess the one thing I could say about my hellish time in Harmony was it met my goal of unpredictability. I studied myself in the mirror one last time, trying to push a wet wiry strand off my forehead. Now, if I could just do something about my hair.

Stuffing my filthy clothes into a plastic bag, I took one last look over V.A.'s bathroom to make sure it was suitable for company. I threw my purse over my shoulder and started down the hall, hoping to escape before the arrival of the book club. No such luck. Filling the entrance to the hallway was a chambray-shirted, denim-covered backside that I prayed was not Noah. Noticing the familiar looking cowboy boots, I groaned inwardly. It was definitely Noah. Darn. At least this time I didn't smell like a high school boys' locker room. "Uh, excuse me," I said, halting the conversation between him and a woman blocked from my view.

Turning around, a look of uncertainty momentarily crossed his face before his mouth turned up at the edges. "No hat."

"Huh?"

"The baseball cap you had on earlier."

"Oh." I reached my free hand up and touched my hair. "No. Uh, V.A. let me use her shower." I gestured toward the closed bathroom door.

"I can see that." He reached out and touched his index finger to my ear.

I recoiled, wondering what in the hell he was doing.

"Soap." He held his finger up, his eyes crinkling into a smile. "Colorful."

Sure enough there was a purple glob clinging to his finger. "It's for the red." I grabbed my ears one at a time searching for any more shampoo remnants.

"The red?"

"Yeah, purple for red hair, blue for blonde. It keeps it from looking dull." My God, what kind of bizarre talk was this to be having with a cowboy?

"It seems to be working." He scanned his eyes over my hair.

"Yeah, the Grandpa Roberts curse, I'm afraid." I noticed a pair of curious eyes looking over Noah's shoulder. Time to move along, but Noah seemed in no hurry to let me by.

"You sure wouldn't get lost in a crowd."

"Thanks." Jeez the guy was a real enchanter. "I should be going." I started to nudge my way around him.

"You're welcome to stay."

"I don't think I'd contribute much since I haven't read the book."

"You've probably read this one. It's *The Scarlet Letter*."

"Really? That seems a strange choice for a book club."

"We like to take on one classic piece of literature a year. They make for some of our best discussions." He swatted the novel against his hand.

"Well, it's been far too long since I've read it. I'm going to have to pass." This time, I made it all the way around him, but the tight squeeze brought me close enough to smell that male blend of musk, soap, and freshly-shaven skin. Delectable. Why does that smell always suck me in? I had to stop myself from taking a deep breath.

CHAPTER FIVE

Making my way back toward Cal's, the first pangs of hunger were starting to hit, but the thought of dining in my RV on bag salad while enjoying a view of the junkyard had no appeal. I decided to stop in at Dusty's. How bad could it be?

Stepping across the green linoleum floor, I quickly made my way to the counter. Even at thirty-three years old, I had not mastered the art of sitting alone at a restaurant table without feeling awkward, unless I had my nose buried in a book pretending to be totally engrossed.

The layout of the place was classic diner. Beyond the collection of tables and booths, it had a counter with a few well-worn swivel stools overlooking a work area stacked with thick coffee mugs and plates. A pass-through above a stainless steel shelf offered a view of a generous torso wrapped in a stained white apron with a hairy arm wielding a spatula. I checked to my right and left, half expecting to see Dagwood Bumstead. Nope. Just an older gentleman in a plaid shirt, whose conversation with the waitress dubbed him a regular.

When she made her way over to me after topping off a cup of coffee for the local, I was surprised to see that the waitress's attire was much more Santa Monica coffee house than Harmony diner. Woven into her long dark hair were strands of turquoise feathers and multi-colored ribbons, and the edge of a tattoo was just visible above the u-shaped neckline of her black knit top.

As she placed a menu in front of me, I caught the light of curiosity in her eyes, quickly overshadowed by practiced indifference. She took my drink order of iced tea, and I had just begun to read the menu when Deputy Crane slid onto the stool next to mine.

"Thought that was you." He glanced over at me while adjusting his service belt. He was carrying a gun, nothing unusual for a cop, but somehow still menacing. "Your red hair is hard to miss."

"So I've been told." These comments on my hair color were making me feel like I had regressed to the elementary school playground. A girl could get a complex if she stayed around Harmony long enough. "Any recommendations?" I held up the menu.

"You can't go wrong with most anything Dusty cooks. He does a great job with the buffalo."

"As in, *give me a home where the buffalo roam*? That kind of buffalo?"

"Yeah. My favorite's the buffalo Bolognese."

"Really? But isn't that kinda like eating spotted owl or something."

"No," he said in a patient tone. "Their numbers will never reach anywhere near what they were, but they've been making a comeback for quite a while, and there are ranchers who raise them as livestock."

"Well okay then, I guess it's the buffalo Bolognese." I set the menu down while trying to shut out the chorus of *Home on the Range* already circling my brain.

With the buffalo lesson exhausted and our meals ordered, I wondered if Deputy Crane would mind talking about spouse abuser Samuel Vaullie while off duty. I decided to test the waters by easing into the subject. "Have you lived in Harmony all your life, Deputy?" I asked.

"No. I was raised in St. George." He pushed his glasses up the bridge of his nose. "I went away to college, did my undergrad at Gonzaga in Eastern Washington and my graduate degree at the University of Washington."

So that's why the guy didn't have the looks of your typical small town deputy—at least not the stereotypes on the boob tube. "So, how'd you end up, you know?" I looked over my shoulder out the window to Main Street.

"You mean, what in the heck am I doing in Harmony, Utah?" His eyes softened and crinkled up at the corners.

"Yeah." I smiled and raised my shoulders. "What in the heck are you doing in Harmony, Utah?"

"My major was criminal justice, but my real interest is cold cases. After school, I spent six years on the police force in Tacoma working homicide. With all the paperwork, I didn't have the time to dedicate to my cold cases, so I quit and took the position here." Fiddling with his fork and spoon, he continued, "Harmony is pretty quiet, so I can do my job *and* work on my investigations."

"Sounds interesting," I said, covering for my incredulity that he couldn't find a small town with a whole lot more to offer than Harmony, where you could spend your free time searching for loose felons.

The waitress set our plates down in front of the deputy and me, halting our conversation. I offered a quick, "Thanks." As I stared at the meaty red sauce I was having doubts about my order, that is, until I took my first bite. "Oh my God, this is amazing," I said to no one in particular.

My response brought the torso in the kitchen over to the pass-through, and as he bent down to see who was making the fuss over his food, the face above the apron finally came out of hiding. It was ruddy, but clean-shaven, open, and friendly. "Your first time for buffalo?"

"Yeah. There's not a lot of call for it in L.A." When he looked at me questioningly, I continued quickly, "It really is terrific. It's so tender, and the pasta is fantastic."

"Made to order."

"You're kidding."

"I don't kid about food, Missy." He smiled and stepped away from the window.

Again with the Missy. Wow. Who was he, V.A.'s brother?

After coming through the kitchen door, he stepped behind the counter. "Dried pasta ruins a dish like this. It has to be fresh."

"Remarkable." I wondered how discerning the town folk's taste buds really were, especially in light of Cal's whole bear hunting proclivity. Hoping that Dusty had not read my thoughts, I extended my hand. "Hi. I'm Sydney Roberts."

"Dusty Dufrain." He wiped his hand on his apron before he took mine.

"Nice to meet you."

"Crane." Dusty nodded his head in the deputy's direction.

The deputy, now focused entirely on his meal, pulled himself away from it just long enough to offer a quick return nod.

"If you like this dish, you need to come back on Friday. I do buffalo steaks, with corn on the cob, the whole works."

Deputy Crane concurred with a mumbled mouthful, "Best thing you'll ever eat."

"It sounds great, but I'll be long gone by then. I'm only here until Cal gets my RV fixed."

"Cal, huh?"

"Yeah, the parts are supposed to be here by tomorrow."

"I'll save a steak for you, just in case. Enjoy the Bolognese. Gotta get back to my duties." Dusty winked and disappeared into the kitchen.

I had that sinking feeling back in my stomach. It sounded like Dusty had about as much faith in Cal as V.A.

When I saw that the deputy was almost through with his meal, I decided I should table any talk about Samuel Vaullie to the next day. "I'd like to come by the station tomorrow morning, if you don't mind."

Signaling to the waitress that he was ready for his check, he responded, "It's only been a few hours since you filed your report, a bit soon to have caught the bad guys."

"Oh no, it's not about that. I want to talk to you about Samuel Vaullie, you know, the polygamist who lives outside of town."

The waitress, who had come over and was tearing our checks from her pad, stopped and focused her attention on us. Ignoring her, I continued, "I want to see about filing a report about the way he has been treating his child bride, Ruthie."

"That's a mighty sticky area."

"So, I've been told, but I'd like to discuss it with you anyway."

"Well then, come on by." He took the check from the waitress.

"Nine o'clock okay?"

"Sure." He put his payment down and slid it across the counter to the waitress. "Thanks, Dori. See you tomorrow." As he was going out the door, he passed Lloyd and Floyd Bailey and two of their equally scroungy friends, who were shuffling in. "Boys," I heard him say as he placed his hat on his head. They didn't respond with a word or gesture. They just slid into the nearest booth and assumed the slouching position mandated by their ilk.

Shaking my head at them, I turned back and the waitress was still standing there, my check in her hand. She had an indecisive look on her face, puzzling considering it didn't take a lot of mental acuity to total a restaurant tab. "I'd like to pay for my dinner."

"Oh yeah, sure," she said, but just stood there. Lowering her voice, she scanned the restaurant. "I want to talk to you about Samuel Vaullie. Would you mind having some dessert and coffee on me and waiting until things clear out a bit around here?"

Hmm. Well, that was interesting twist. But then, what else did I have to do? "Okay." I shrugged my shoulders.

As I was eating the berry pie that Dori brought me, I took a good look at the bus boy, who had been working the tables all evening in such a quiet manner that he almost went unnoticed. He had Dori's same dark hair and light skin. It appeared as if they could be related, so I asked, "Your brother?" glancing at him over my shoulder as Dori poured me another half cup of coffee.

"Yeah, that's Luke, how'd you know?"

"You look a lot alike. Is this a family business? Is Dusty your dad?"

"No. He just gave us these jobs when we were looking for work. He's a good guy."

"Seems like it."

"Darn them!" Dori focused in on the Bailey boys' table. They had finished their burgers and were flinging the fries at each other across the table. Most of them were landing on the floor. "The little twerps." Walking out from behind the counter, she made a beeline for their booth. "Cut it out, right now!" I heard her command.

"Why should we?" one of the twins sneered at her.

"Because if you don't, I'll have your asses kicked out of here."

"Ooh, like we really care," the other twin said, picking up where his brother left off. "We're leavin' this grease pit anyway."

"Not soon enough for me." Dori looked over at the next booth as she spoke, noticing that one of the diners was motioning to her with his coffee cup.

As Dori walked back to grab the coffee pot, her brother approached the Bailey boys' table to begin clearing the dishes.

"Hey, Luuuke," one of the friends said, drawing out the "u" sound in his name. He was echoed by the other boys chanting, "Luke, Luke, Luke, Luke."

Luke kept his head down, not making any eye contact with them. When he reached for a glass on the far side of the table, one of the twins slid it away and snickered. "Can't reach it,

Luuuke? Here, let me help you." At that, he gave the glass a hard shove and slid it across the table. Trying to grab for it before it fell to the floor, while balancing his tray, Luke knocked it on its side and the remaining contents spilled all over his pants.

The boys began to laugh in a high pitch that revealed their fluctuating hormones, one-upping each other in volume and frenzy.

Luke set the tray down and began to wipe at his pants with a towel he took from his back pocket. "Gotta get this off. Gotta get this off. Gotta get this off," he repeated, which drove the boys into greater fits of hysteria.

"What a freak," one of the twins said between laughs.

Tossing his head from side to side, Luke dropped the towel, clapped his hands over his ears and muttered over and over, "Too loud; too loud; too loud; too loud."

Dori was back at their booth in two seconds, clutching the coffee pot in a white-knuckled fist. Gesturing with the pot, her face contorted with fury, she yelled, "Get out! Now!" The coffee slopped out of the pot precariously close to one of the twin's greasy head.

"Hey, watch it, bitch!" He ducked back. "You burn me, and my mom will sue you."

"Out! Out! Out!" Dori slapped her free hand on the table.

By this time Dusty had come out of the kitchen, and I had jumped off my chair, wanting to slap the little beasts silly.

The boys slowly made their way out of the booth under Dori's glare, feigning nonchalance, or maybe they weren't feigning. Maybe they weren't feeling any remorse or fear at all. Maybe they were completely devoid of shame. Scary.

Dusty followed them to the door. "It's best you stay away from here," he said as he opened it to let them out.

"No problem, old man. We don't need this dump."

Dori had put the coffee pot down and was talking quietly to her brother. "Lucas, pull your hands off your ears," she said. "They're gone now. Come sit over in your corner." She put her head very close to his face, but didn't touch him. "Lucas. Come on now. Open your eyes, and let's go to the corner."

Luke opened his eyes and dropped his arms to his side, and with a few whispered urges from Dori finally followed her to the booth in the corner. When he sat down, she grabbed a fleece jacket from the seat and helped Lucas into it. He folded his arms and began to rock slightly. "Lucas, no rocking," Dori said. "Please try to sit still while I bring you an ice cream."

"Vanilla. I only eat vanilla," he said.

"Yes, I know, Lucas. I'll bring vanilla."

"Two scoops, side by side, not on top of each other."

"Yes, I know, Lucas, two scoops, side by side." Dori walked into the kitchen.

Still standing in the middle of the room, I looked around at the other diners. They had returned to their eating, apparently not too disturbed by the events of the last few minutes.

"Can I get you another piece of pie," Dusty asked as he also headed toward the kitchen, motioning me back to the counter.

"No. I'm good." I walked over to my stool and sat back down, a little confused by the lack of interest displayed over what I thought was a highly disturbing episode. Peeking back over my shoulder at Luke, I saw that he was still holding his arms tightly around his chest, staring at the table. Emerging from the kitchen, Dori walked quickly across the room, placed the ice cream down in front of him and set a spoon next to it.

Luke began humming as he took his first bite.

"Try not to hum, Lucas," I heard her say. "It's over now. Our shift is almost done, and when we get home you can finish your computer project."

"Yes. I earned ninety minutes. You remember, ninety minutes."

"Yes, I remember. I'm going to get back to work now, Lucas. When you're through with your ice cream, finish clearing the tables, okay."

"Okay. I will do that. Okay."

"Good."

After the last of the diners left the restaurant, Dori came over and sat down on the stool next to mine. She glanced over at Luke, who was sitting at the booth playing a handheld video game. I followed her gaze, and when I looked back at her I was hoping for some kind of explanation about what was going on with him. Nosey, I know. But that's me.

"I overheard you talking to Deputy Crane about Samuel Vaullie," she said. Apparently Dori was not going to talk about her brother, and apparently she wasn't big on segueing into conversations by exchanging introductions.

"Yes."

"How do you know him?" She swiveled on her chair, so that she was facing me.

"I don't actually. I stumbled upon his house when my RV broke down, then ran into him again when Ruthie was at the dentist's office."

"Then what makes you think he's abusing her?" She stared at me inquisitively through dark eyes.

"Wait a minute. Let's back up a little, shall we." I decided to put a halt to what already was feeling like an interrogation, at least long enough to find out a little bit about her, and what direction she was headed with her probing. "Other than your first name and that you have a brother, I don't know anything about you, and I'm not really comfortable talking about a subject like this with a stranger."

"Sorry. I've been told I'm really focused–a nice word for intense. I'm Dori Hunt." She held out her hand.

"Sydney Roberts." I shook it.

"You're not from Utah, right?"

"L.A., or formerly L.A., I should say."

"As soon as my brother and I are able, that's where we're headed."

"Why?" I gave her a skeptical glance.

"Have you looked around here? Not exactly paradise. The beaches of Southern California sound a whole lot better. That, and being able to get lost in the crowd."

"Well, it's definitely the right place if you're looking for crowds–any time of the day or night."

Dori hesitated, pulling on her bottom lip, then said, "Look, I know we should make more small talk before going on with the conversation about Samuel Vaullie, but I need to get my brother home pretty soon, so would you mind if we just get to the point?"

"No, I guess not." I shrugged.

"Why are you bothering to talk to Crane about Samuel?" she asked. "You're not moving here, right?"

"No. God, no." I frowned.

"Did you actually see him abuse her?"

"When they were at V.A.'s, he grabbed her by the arm and shoved her into his truck, just because I talked to her. I don't know if that qualifies as abuse, but it sure seemed like it to me. And, he's probably three times her age! He had to have forced himself on her, taken advantage of her innocence and immaturity. She can't even be sixteen, can she? It's disgusting." Recalling my two meetings with Samuel started to get me fired up again. "What's your interest in him?"

"He's only one of dozens of creeps in Utah, Arizona, Canada, Mexico, and other places who use their religion to defend their sicko behavior! They prey on children; they brainwash their wives; they destroy lives; and they get away with it!"

"Cal and V.A. didn't seem all that concerned."

"Polygamist groups are crawling with pedophiles and sadists who beat their wives and children every day! And, as for the folks around here, they're just like people everywhere— too darn caught up in their own lives to do anything about it!"

"Law enforcement has to be aware of men like Samuel Vaullie. It's their job."

"Sure they are, but because they've had so little success dealing with them, I think they'd just rather not be bothered."

"Even though these sickos lure young women into having sex with them in the name of some self-serving definition of marriage?"

"Even though. There's a history, you know, of cops gathering enough evidence against polygamists to make a good case against them, then having the whole thing crap out. Most people don't have the stomach to watch children be taken from their mothers. Polygamists count on that. Warren

Jeffs' arrest helped some. It took a long time, though, and video evidence of him in bed with underage girls before he was convicted!" Dori's eyes flashed.

"Wow," I sighed, leaning my elbow on the counter. "Then nothing can be done about Samuel Vaullie's grip on Ruthie."

"If there was nothing that could be done, I would have slit my wrists years ago." The dark tone in Dori's voice made it sound like that statement was not hyperbole. "No. I'm not saying that at all." She angled her tensed body slightly toward me. "There's a small but growing group of us who are not going to shut up until something is done to help the victims of polygamy escape from these bastards. So, back to my original question; what's your interest in all this?"

I had to think about that one. Why was I involving myself in the lives of people who would be a shrinking image in my rearview mirror in a day or two? "I guess I find Samuel Vaullie's behavior so disturbing I want to at least put it on record in the event that someone finally decides to do something about it."

"Believe me, there are people who intend to do something about it, but Crane probably isn't one of them."

"I don't know. He doesn't seem like the type to shirk his responsibilities."

"Don't get me wrong. He's actually a good deputy sheriff and a great guy, but like I said, cops don't want to take a stand. With such a high failure rate in convictions, they think these cases will come back to bite them on their asses. Basically, Samuel Vaullie would have to rape one of his wives in the middle of Main Street with twenty-five eyewitnesses and a news crew before the authorities would feel confident about making an arrest!"

"That's putting it bluntly."

"That's the truth." She frowned.

"It really irks me to let that devil ride rough shod over his group without doing something."

"There's plenty you could do, if you were sticking around."

"But, I'm not."

"Too bad. We could use your anger."

Anger? Where'd she get that one? "I'm not angry. I just don't like injustice."

"No. You're angry. It's written all over your face. And, you'd be right there with us if you lived here." Popping up from the stool, she started toward Luke. "It's been nice knowing ya." She raised her hand in good-bye.

Wow. With that dismissal, it seemed my usefulness was over. "Wait. Who's us?" I called after her.

"A group of twelve angry women. You'd fit right in." She looked back at me.

CHAPTER SIX

In that muddled state between sleep and wakefulness, I couldn't remember where I was. Opening my eyes a slit, I stared dumbly at the window blinds. They looked vaguely familiar, but definitely not like the ones in the apartment. Tapping my hands around the blanket, I finally found what I was looking for–Alice's body was curled up at the edge of the bed. She purred when I stroked her. "Where are we, girl?" I said out loud. Then in two heartbeats, I remembered. I groaned and laid the back of my arm over my eyes, thinking, Oh, God, I'm still here in a junkyard in Harmony. Cal damn well better know something about those parts, or my cousin Ralph may just have to do without Uncle George's RV, even if I have to walk to New York!

After dressing and having breakfast, I decided to empty Alice's litter box and find Cal. I also thought I had better check in with Mr. Bumbles–I had hardly seen him in the last two days. Harmony may have been hell for me, but Bumbles was having the time of his life.

Picking my way through the yard, I was having a hard time finding a dumpster–but then, the entire place could qualify. I finally found Cal with his head so far into the engine compartment of a beater truck his feet barely touched the ground. "Do you have some place I could throw this litter away?" I asked, careful not to brush up against the truck.

Cal's head jerked up and he banged it on the hood of the truck. "Ouch!" He rubbed it as he turned around. "Don't you know not to sneak up on a man when he's working on a vehicle? You gotta give a body some warning."

"Sorry." I grimaced. "Can I get you some ice or something?"

"Nah, it'll be all right. He continued to rub it with a hand that was black with grease. Dark hair is certainly an advantage for someone in Cal's profession.

"I'm looking for someplace to throw this." I held up the bag of litter. "If you don't mind."

"You can toss it in with the dog shit right there in that can." He nodded to a dented aluminum trash bin, circa 1940, a few feet away.

Oh good. I got to begin the morning by opening the lid on a can of coonhound shit. "Thanks," then added, "Did you hear from the parts supplier in Salt Lake last night?"

"Nope. They close at six."

"How about this morning?"

"Nope. They open at nine."

"Do you plan on calling them when they open?" My voice was taking on an edge.

Cal dropped his hand from his head and leveled a suspicious gaze at me. "Soon after."

"How soon after?" I tried to make my voice sound light.

"I'll finish what I'm doing here and that will make it soon after they open."

Great. Cal probably had zero sense of time, so I offered, "How about if I call them?"

"And say what exactly?"

"You already ordered the parts, right? I can call and check on the order."

"Nah." Cal fished around in his shirt pocket, pulled out a toothpick and twirled it between his fingers. "It's best if you leave it to me, with your temper and all."

"My temper!" I could have chucked the litterbag right at him.

"Yeah. Like that. Your ornery tone won't sit well with them up there."

Oh my God! Who was he buying the parts from, the mafia? I stared him down while weighing my options and decided to give it the morning before making any rash decisions regarding the motorhome—or strangling Cal with my bare hands. Between gritted teeth, I said, "I'm going to walk into town and grab a few things. I'll check in with you when I get back to find out what they had to say."

He just nodded as he stuck the toothpick between his molars.

And I headed for the shit can.

On my way out of Cal's yard, I spied Mr. Bumbles with his buddies and decided to grab his leash from the RV and take him with me on my walk into town. It was still early enough that the air was cool on my skin and it had a pungent smell—sage, I guessed. From the way Mr. B was loping along beside me, his tags jingling as we made our way up Main Street, I could tell he was in a particularly perky mood.

Actually, I don't believe I have ever met a bad-tempered Basset Hound. It's just not in their DNA.

Filing my report on Samuel Vaullie with Deputy Crane didn't take much time, but made me feel better. Although the deputy probably thought my report was a waste of ink, he behaved like a man who took his job seriously, cold case or not.

Leaving his office, I decided I had better stop in at V.A.'s to let her know I planned on keeping my Wednesday appointment to have my chipped tooth fixed. As much as I hated to admit it, it was the one good thing about my delayed departure, because I was having a hell of a time keeping my tongue off the break in my tooth. Ignoring little irritants like hangnails and paper cuts is not my strong suit.

V.A.'s screen door was locked up tight, and it took several knocks before she answered. "What can I do for you, Missy?" she asked, keeping the door between us.

I guess I was stuck with the Missy thing. "I just wanted to let you know I will definitely be here tomorrow morning for my appointment."

"That's fine."

"Office not open today?" I peered over her shoulder into the dark room.

"My mother called from the ranch. She needs some help with a calving, so I had to shuffle my appointments around." Looking down, she noticed Mr. Bumbles, who had used the opportunity to stretch out on his side. Why sit when you can lie down, that's his philosophy. "Who's this fella?" she asked, her eyes lighting up.

"Mr. Bumbles."

"Ha!" She laughed. "Great name. I thought you folks from California favored those puny purse dogs."

Jeez, those entertainment news shows sure didn't do much for the ordinary Californian's reputation. "No," I answered. "There are a lot of us out there with dogs that don't fit in purses."

"Ha!" She blasted her laugh again, this time loud enough to raise Mr. B to a sitting position. "Well, he looks like a dandy."

"A real sweetheart." I rubbed my hand over the knot on his head. Bumbles smiled, his tongue raining droplets of drool over V.A.'s porch.

"He looks thirsty. Let me grab him a bowl of water, then I have to take off."

"That'd be great," I said, thankful for the offer. Cool morning or not, it was a desert dry place, and we still had to stop at the store and walk back to the RV.

Stepping through her squeaky door and out onto the porch, V.A. set the bowl down. Mr. B noisily lapped up the water, making sure to thoroughly douse his ears in the process. She stroked his back, then straightened up. Hand on the screen door, she asked, "What are you doing today?"

"Just waiting for the parts for the RV to come in so Cal can get it fixed."

"How about riding along with me to the ranch? I may need an extra hand with the calving."

I didn't see that one coming. "I ... um," I stuttered, "I don't know that I would be much help to you. The closest I have ever been to a cow is at the butcher shop."

She waved off my concern. "You look sturdy. You'll do fine."

Okay, I know that I'm tall, but sturdy? That's like calling someone a big buxom woman. My self-image was on a serious downhill slide.

Once again, V.A. had little patience for my hesitation. "Time's wasting, Missy."

Why not ride out to the ranch with her? The idea of this move was to get out of my rut, and a calving, whatever that entailed, would certainly qualify. "Sure," I said, "I'll go, but what about him?" I patted Mr. B's head.

"Bring him along."

"But his drooling makes a mess of car windows."

"I drive a truck. He'll ride in the back."

Apparently Mr. Bumbles was moving out of his rut too.

After a fifteen-minute ride down a mostly deserted highway, we turned onto a dirt road, and V.A. pulled the truck up to a rusty gate. "You mind?" she nodded at the gate.

"No." I popped out of the truck, swung it open, and closed it after she went through, making sure it was shut tight. From the way Mr. Bumbles was watching, his tail beating hard against the truck bed, I could tell he thought this was pretty cool stuff.

"Were you raised on this ranch?" I asked V.A., as we bounced our way over the rutted lane toward a house and barn that were about a quarter mile off in the distance.

"Yup. I was born right here."

Looking around at the mostly arid landscape, not seeing evidence of much activity, I asked, "What do you grow here?"

"We don't grow anything, except a little feed and a small garden for our personal use. We raise cattle. The ranch is five thousand acres."

"Wow. Your herd must be huge."

"Not really. This is pretty poor land. It takes a whole lot of it to support a few cattle."

As we drove closer to the dwellings, V.A. turned down the path that led to the barn and parked the truck just short of the open doors. "Let's go see what we got," she said, as she stepped down from the truck.

After jumping out my side, I lowered the truck gate, helped Mr. Bumbles down, and entered the barn. As my eyes adjusted to the change in light, I saw V.A. leaning against the rail of a cattle stall, conferring with a gray-haired woman who almost equaled her in height. At their feet was a large black cow, rasping out a mournful low every few seconds. When she saw me, V.A. waved me over. "Sydney, this is my mother, Miriam."

How about that? V.A. did know my name. "Hello," I said, noting that the similarity between the two women extended to their blue-gray eyes as well as their height.

"And that's Mr. Bumbles." V.A. smiled and nodded in his direction.

Miriam smiled also. "Nice to meet you both."

"She's not doing too well, huh?" I stared down at the cow, in awe of the girth from her pregnancy and her size in general. She looked so much bigger than the ones on milk cartons.

"No, she's not," V.A. answered. "Mama says she's been straining for several hours now, and nothing's happening. I need to check out what's going on. We're likely to have to pull the calf."

Pull the calf? That couldn't be good. The cow lowed again and shifted its weight. Looking down at it, I wondered what part V.A. had in mind for me in the whole pull the calf thing.

Surely she didn't believe I was capable of animal husbandry of any sort beyond feeding and watering.

"I'm afraid you're going to have to get her up first and into the chute. It will be much easier to handle her there," Miriam said, looking at the two of us.

I looked back down at the cow. Get her up? Did she not notice that the cow was in no mood to go anywhere? And did she not notice that the cow outweighed us by one or two tons. What was the matter with me? Why hadn't I ever learned to say, no?

"I'm not going to be of much help, I'm afraid." Miriam massaged one hand with the other. "My arthritis is giving me fits right now."

"That's okay, Mama. We can handle it." V.A. moved around to the front of the cow.

We can? I stared at V.A. Maybe *you* can. You were raised here. I, on the other hand, was not. Twirling Mr. Bumbles' leash in my hands, I looked down at him. He lifted one eyebrow at me. I bet he thought it was really funny. He thumped his tale. Bumbles is not particular about the attention you give him, just so long as he gets some every once in a while.

"Sydney, come on over here and help me while I coax her up," V.A. said.

"What should I do with him?" I asked, gesturing with Bumbles' leash.

"I'll take him," Miriam said.

"He'll probably need to pee." I handed the leash to her. "He hasn't been since we left town."

"Okay, and I'll give him a little water and leave him in the house out of the way." Heading out the barn door, she called back, "I'll meet you at the chute with the Crisco."

Crisco? I didn't even ask.

"What I need you to do," V.A. said, when I joined her by the cow's head, "is pull up and out on the rope while I prod her from the side."

I grabbed the rope, catching a glimpse of a very agitated look in the cow's eyes. She let out a loud low, and I jumped.

"She's not going to hurt you. Just stay out of the way of her hooves."

"No problem there." I took a small step back.

"Come on now, girl." V.A. pushed on the cow's haunches. "Get up." Between her teeth, she said to me, "Tug on the rope, Missy, a good steady pull."

I did as I was told, but it felt like I was trying to move a brick wall. She didn't budge. And, the look in her eyes was quickly morphing from agitated to crazed.

"Okay, let's change places," V.A. said, acknowledging that we were getting nowhere. "Just kinda rock her hind quarters as best as you can."

Getting down on my knees, I clenched my jaw and pushed with all my might, wondering at the plausibility of my moving her even an inch. V.A. was coaxing her with soothing tones, occasionally clucking at her like she was calling a chicken. Whatever works, I guess. I finally felt her shift a little under my hands.

"Good girl," V.A. said, pulling so hard I could see the veins in her arms. "That's it. Get up now."

The cow finally moved to its knees. Do they have knees? And its mountain of hindquarters rose up, knocking me onto my butt. Now eye level with the hooves that V.A. warned me about, I scooted backward through the straw. From the sudden dampness I felt through my jeans and the accompanying stink, I realized that in my haste I had been mopping up cow dung and pee. Lovely.

Standing up, I grabbed a handful of straw and tried my best to scrape it off, but didn't get far before V.A. was giving me more orders. "We need to disinfect her and ourselves," she said, leading her to a washstand on the opposite side of the barn, as I followed behind. "Grab some rubber bands out of that can there." She nodded to one on the ground next to the sink. "And tie up her tail for me, would ya."

Once I had haphazardly coiffed the cow's tail, V.A. said, "Come on around here and hang onto her lead while I get her cleaned up. I don't want to tie her off in the event she tries to go down again."

I was back staring into those huge crazed brown eyes, and her lowing now had taken on a hair-raising intensity. After cleaning the cow's backside, V.A. washed her hands, rolled up the sleeves of her t-shirt, and scrubbed her arms clear up to the pits. "Your turn," she said, grabbing the rope from me. "Be sure to use the brush under your nails, and don't miss the back side of your arms."

Rolling my own t-shirt up, I scrubbed so hard I thought my freckles might come off. No chance.

"Now, we need to move, or that calf's gonna be in trouble."

I followed her out into the bright hot sun of the yard and into a small corral. V.A. quickly led the cow into a chute, closed a gate around her neck, then clamped bars down on either side of her. Wow. That seemed a little harsh for a cow in labor.

"Heifers like the sensation of being closed in." V.A. must have caught the look of disapproval on my face. "Makes 'em feel more secure."

"Here's the Crisco and snares." Miriam stepped into the corral, her arms full. "And you need to wear these hats, girls, or you're going to fry."

Girls? I looked over at V.A. She had already grabbed the Crisco, opened the lid, and was spreading it on her right arm, all the way up. Girl was not exactly the term I would have used for V.A.

Seeing that V.A. was not going to be able to do it herself, Miriam set a worn straw cowboy hat on her head. "Thanks, Mama," V.A. said.

Hearing a six-foot tall woman call her mother *Mama* didn't mesh with the image I had of her any more than her mother calling her a girl, but even V.A. had to have been a mama's girl at one time.

"Here you go." Miriam set the other equally as worn hat on my head, and it actually fit.

"It was my late husband's. I thought it might be big enough for all that red hair of yours."

And the red hair remarks just kept on coming. I guess it was better than commenting on the basketball size of my head.

"Okay, let's see what we got here." V.A. took no time inserting her arm into the cow's birth canal as far as she could reach. I guess I knew that at some point something like that was going to happen, but it was still a shocker to see an arm disappear into a cow. Her face beet red from straining, V.A.

closed her eyes to a slit, "Posterior presentation, for sure, but nothing abnormal. Just a big calf."

"So backward?" I asked, proud of myself for actually knowing a little something about the birth process. "But, isn't that bad?"

"No. Not if the legs or the head aren't bent back. But we have to hurry on this one because it takes that much longer before the calf can get its first breath." Extracting her arm from the cow, she said, "What I'm going to do is snare the legs. We each take one, and when the heifer strains, we pull in a slightly upward direction. Keep in mind we have to pull together in one slow steady motion, and it's a rope, not a two by four. We don't pull unless she's straining, so you wait for my signal. You got all that?"

"Sure." I looked over at Miriam. She nodded at me reassuringly.

After V.A. reached back into the birth canal and placed the snares around the calf's back legs, she wiped the Crisco off her hand. Handing me one of the ropes, she said, "Make sure you have a good grip on it."

"Okay. Got it." I held tight to the rope. At that point, I have to admit, my adrenaline had kicked in, and I was feeling a little earth mama vibe. Like, look at me; I'm pulling a calf. Then V.A. started tugging on some big membraney looking thing at the entrance to the birth canal, while saying, "We have to keep the vulva back so it doesn't tear during the birth." And, as I tried to keep myself from tossing up my breakfast, my two-second earth mama moment ended.

"You ready?" V.A. snapped me to attention. My breakfast was going to have to stay put. "She's straining. Now, pull."

I pulled, and oh my God, V.A. neglected to mention that it was going to be like a game of tug-o-war between a Sumo wrestling team and us. I may look like Amazon woman, but my narrow shoulders and puny arms were nothing like V.A.'s beefy biceps.

"That's it, keep pulling," Miriam encouraged from her post next to us. "You're doing it."

Right. I hadn't felt any movement at all.

"Okay, let up. She stopped straining," V.A. said, giving me a sideways glance. Was she reconsidering the wisdom of asking me to help? "Shake your arms out. Get the blood circulating."

I was happy to do so.

"Okay, good. Now grab the rope. Here we go. Pull."

This time something did give. Letting go with one hand, V.A. moved the vulva away while keeping the pressure on, and two small hooves made their first appearance. Pretty cool. Then they started to slip back out of our grasp. "Hang on, Missy. Don't let go." All the muscles in my arms burned, but I gritted my teeth and held tight.

"Just keep a constant pressure, so we don't lose it, but don't pull until she strains again." Oh boy, no break this time. After a few beats, I could feel the cow tense again. I was finally starting to understand the rhythm. "Pull," V.A. said, and this time both back legs came all the way out.

"With the next strain, I'm going to push on her pelvis while you pull, so you're going to have to handle both legs," V.A. instructed. "Can you do that?"

My arms were starting to shake from the exertion, but I nodded my head. My competitive side had kicked in, and I wasn't about to show weakness in front of V.A.

"Good. Take this, and use the same steady pressure." She handed me her rope. V.A. pulled the vulva out of the way again, and grunting, used all her force to push on the pelvis. We were working so close together, I could see the pores on her face and the rivulets of sweat running down her neck. My hands were perspiring, and I wasn't sure how long I could keep it up. Just about that time, the calf's hindquarters started to appear. "Okay, it's going to go fast now. When the calf comes out, we have to hang on to it and hold it upside down to drain the fluid from its lungs. Give me the second rope, and hang onto yours, but with your other hand get a good grip on the leg. And whatever you do, don't drop it. Ready now. Pull!"

Wet from the birth canal, the calf slid completely out, and suddenly it was dead weight in my hand, a lot of it. Losing my grip, I panicked. "Whoa! Help!" I called out, and dropped the rope so I could hold onto the leg with both hands. It was too slick, and quickly slipping from my grasp. "Oh, no," I gasped, as I teetered, losing my footing in the bloody-looking gunk that had accumulated underneath us. "I can't hang on!" At that moment, two large hands reached around me and grabbed the calf's leg. Good thing too, for the next thing I knew I was flat on my back, staring blindly into the cowboy hat.

Moaning from the throbbing pain in my tailbone, I picked the hat off my face, just as a blur of denim-clad legs and a lifeless calf passed over me. Planting my elbow in the filthy straw, I rolled on one butt cheek to a sitting position to see what was happening.

"That's right. Let's get him on this pile of clean straw," Miriam said, as V.A. and a cowboy whose backside looked vaguely familiar carried the calf over to her. "Let me make sure his lungs are clear before you set him down." She knelt to reach the calf's head. After running her hand in his mouth and over his nose, she grabbed a handful of straw and began vigorously rubbing his chest. "Did you see any fluid drain from him," she asked, looking up at V.A.

"Yep. Quite a bit right at first."

"Then go ahead and lie him down now. And bring his mama over while I tend to him."

"I'll get her," the cowboy said, hurrying toward the chute.

As he came closer I realized it was Noah. Of course. I looked around for the white stallion he rode in on.

Stopping beside me, he stared straight down, with that damn twinkle in his eyes. "You need to move." He reached his hand out.

I took it and let him help me up, but only because I was going to have a tough time doing it on my own. "Thanks." I met that twinkle with an offhand glance. Turning, I winced and stifled a moan, picked up the hat, and walked over to V.A. and Miriam with as normal a gait as I could muster. Jeez. First my ankle and tooth, then my tailbone. I should have taken up prizefighting instead of cross-country travel. It's a lot safer.

V.A. and Miriam were still rubbing the calf from head to toe. "Is it alive?" I asked, not seeing any movement.

"Sure is," Miriam answered.

"How can you tell?"

"He's been batting his eyelashes at us. See there," she said, as the calf picked his head up off the straw. "He'll be a whole lot livelier just as soon as he smells his mama."

"Oh, my gosh. Look at that." The calf's struggle to make his first movements mesmerized me. Ignoring my pain, I crouched down to get a closer view. So that was the miracle of birth. I reached out to rub my hand over his still wet coat. Amazing. The impact of witnessing it could not be underrated.

"Here you go." Noah stepped up behind us with the cow in tow. She looked quite remarkable for just having popped out a baby the size of a third-grader, and with hooves.

Standing and grabbing the lead, Miriam said, "Thanks, Noah," and pulled the cow to the calf. Goaded by the cow's licking and sniffing, it was only a few minutes before the calf was up on wobbly legs and bobbing along his mother's flank searching for the milk source. Acting like it no longer wanted to be bothered, the cow started to shift away. "Oh no, you don't." Miriam held her to her spot. V.A. guided the calf's head until it found a teat.

Running her hand along the cow's neck, Miriam said, "They're going to be fine now. We just need to wait a few minutes to make sure the calf gets plenty of colostrum, then we can start cleaning up."

Looking down at my slime-splattered t-shirt, I imagined if I looked that bad from the front my backside must be a disaster. And, the smell ... I was hoping it was more the cow than me. I turned to check out my shit-covered butt. No. It was me.

When I looked back up, there was Noah grinning at me.

Glad that you find me so entertaining, I wanted to say to him, but turned to Miriam instead. "Cleaning up sounds great." I pulled out on my sticky t-shirt.

"I meant the corral and barn. Can't leave that kinda mess to fester. You end up with a sick herd."

"Oh sure." I reddened, purposely keeping my eyes off Noah. "What would you like me to do?"

"We'll take care of it all, Mama," V.A. interjected, straightening the hat on her head. "Just follow me, Missy." V.A. strutted toward the chute.

Oh boy. We're having fun now.

CHAPTER SEVEN

Smelling like a scout troop after a ten-day campout, I followed V.A. through the back door of the ranch house and into a large mudroom, wondering how much longer I'd be working on the chain gang before I earned my release.

"You can drop your clothes right there." She pointed to a spot on the worn wood floor in front of the washing machine.

"Excuse me?" I flushed from my neck to my hairline.

"Drop your clothes there. I'll go get showered and changed, then I'll throw our duds in the washer."

"But I don't have anything to change into."

"Oh, that's right." She looked around the room. Walking over to a set of wooden hooks, she grabbed a faded blue jumpsuit, "Throw this on 'til your shower, then I'll get you a robe."

"Okay?" I said to her disappearing back. Craning my ears for the sound of voices, I quickly peeled out of my clothes, stepped into the jumpsuit, and started to zip it up. Stuck. Damn. Hearing the sound of footsteps, I clenched the front of the jumpsuit tight in my hands.

"You all right in there?" Miriam called through the door to the kitchen.

Opening it a crack, I said, "I can't seem to get the zipper up."

"Oh, that hasn't worked in years. Solomon was just too hard on it."

"Solomon?"

"My husband. I'll grab you some safety pins."

The hairs on the back of my neck would have stood up if they hadn't been plastered to my skin with sweat. Miriam had said that the hat she loaned me was her *late* husband's, as in dead. And my naked flesh was currently in full contact with an item of his clothing. Creepy!

When Miriam returned with the safety pins, I said a weak, "Thanks," and pulled the door closed. After pinning the gap as best I could, I stood there, trying not to move, thinking that somehow my skin wouldn't rub into the cloth as much if I stayed still.

"Can I be of some help?" Miriam again asked through the door.

"No, I'm good."

"Well then, come on into the kitchen and let me get you something to drink. You have to be thirsty."

"Have a seat." She gestured to an old maple table and chairs as I stepped into the sun-drenched room.

"I'd just as soon stand, if you don't mind." There was no way I was sitting down in Solomon's jumpsuit, and I also wasn't sure if I was ready to test out my throbbing tailbone.

"Suit yourself. Lemonade?"

"Sure. Thanks."

After an interminably long time making small talk with Miriam while she bustled about the kitchen, V.A. finally returned. "Shower's free. There's a robe hanging on the back of the bathroom door."

"Where's the bathroom?"

"Through the living room, down the hall, first door on your right."

"Lunch will be ready in about fifteen minutes," Miriam added.

"Great." Trying not to trip on the hem of Solomon's jumpsuit, I walked through the door to the living room. When I looked up from my feet, it took me a few seconds to comprehend the scene before me. Across the room was a white-haired old woman, with a walker on one side of her and Mr. Bumbles on the other, who was thoroughly enjoying the way she was stroking his head. Across from them, sitting in a large rocker, was Noah. The conversation they had been having stopped when I entered the room, and their eyes quickly fell to the front of my jumpsuit, which had gaped open at my midriff. Quickly gripping the fabric, I stood rooted to my spot. "Just heading to the shower," I gestured toward the hall across the room with my free hand, the sleeve of the jumpsuit completely covering my arm in Dwarf Dopey fashion.

Shit, there went that mocking grin on Noah's face–again. And I was in no mood for it. "Excuse me." I tugged on one pant leg while continuing to hold tight to the jumpsuit as I shuffled my way across the room. I knew I was being rude in not making eye contact with any of them, including Mr. Bumbles, or introducing myself to the old lady, but to hell with manners. I needed to get out from under their stares and into the bathroom–STAT!

Catching a glimpse of myself in the medicine cabinet mirror, I scowled in disgust at my broken tooth, hat hair, and cow-gunk-smudged face. I was a real beaut, and an impolite one at that.

After my shower, my lingering embarrassment had me contemplating taking up permanent residence in the bathroom, but my hunger finally won out. It had been a long time and a lot of manual labor since breakfast. Dressed only in V.A.'s worn chenille robe and my wet sprung-sprocket hair, out I went for another dose of humiliation.

"There you are," Miriam said, as I entered the kitchen. They were all seated around the table, quietly concentrating on filling their plates from serving dishes mounded with enough food to satiate a fire department. I noticed that Mr. Bumbles had taken his seat on the floor next to the old woman. Traitor.

I followed the aroma of onions and bacon to the empty chair between V.A. and Miriam. That put me right across from Noah, who winked at me in greeting, still with the smile on his face, but not quite as sardonic. What was with the wink? I quickly turned my attention away from Noah to the old woman, hoping to make amends for our first encounter. "We weren't introduced. I'm Sydney Roberts."

Instead of meeting my eyes, she was staring at my chest. Looking down to see what was the matter, I discovered that the robe had worked loose when I sat down, and the top of one breast was slightly exposed. Tugging the robe closed and pulling hard on the tie around my waist, I noticed Noah was staring too. When he saw I had caught him, it was finally his turn to look uncomfortable. I shrugged my shoulders at him, thinking, it's really not that interesting, just your average boob.

"This is Ma Odelia," V.A. spoke up for the woman.

"Nice to meet you."

"Yuh," she said through her nose. I guessed that was hello.

Grabbing my plate, I started to pick up a serving fork and stab a pork chop for myself, when Miriam said, "Now that you're at the table, we can say Grace."

"Right." I put the fork back down.

Looking up under my eyelashes about three minutes into the protracted prayer, I scanned the group. Eyes closed, they were deep into it, even Noah.

There was little conversation during the meal, mostly pass the potatoes comments. Fine by me. After the morning I'd had, all that comfort food tasted so good I could have hummed. And I almost did when Miriam brought out the apple crisp and ice cream. Butter-soaked oat crumbs over stacks of cinnamon-spiced apple slices–yum, yum. When Miriam asked if I'd like seconds, I didn't hesitate. It helped that I was wearing a robe–no expanding waistline threatening to pop the button on my jeans. I decided right then that I needed to eat in my robe more often.

Looking over at V.A. and Miriam, who had also taken seconds, I realized I liked these Utah women. No competing for Miss Cardboard Cutout of the Year here.

When the meal was over, V.A. disappeared into the mudroom to move our clothes into the dryer, and I offered to help with the dishes, but Miriam said I was company and for me to go on into the living room with Noah and Ma Odelia.

Why the "company" etiquette didn't apply to cleaning up cow crap, I don't know.

"Hey, Buddy." I stroked Mr. Bumbles' head on our way into the living room. He looked up at me with his red-rimmed eyes, then trotted over to where Noah was helping Odelia into her chair. I would like to have been mad at Mr. B for his disloyalty, but I knew that with his kind heart, he sensed his presence gave Odelia pleasure. I guessed she was approaching eighty and thought from the way she cradled her left arm perhaps she had had a stroke. I didn't think her speech was slurred much, but like the rest of them, she hardly said anything while we were eating.

Settling into the worn floral couch cushion, I waited until Noah took his position in the rocking chair to ask, "How is it that you showed up just at the right time when we were pulling the calf?"

"Miriam called me when she saw that the heifer was going to be a handful." He brushed the hair away from his eyes with his forearm. "Mine's the next ranch over."

"She was *that* all right." I shifted on the cushion while thinking that the hard maple kitchen chairs had not helped my tailbone one bit.

"You sore?" Noah asked, nodding toward my derriere.

"No." Did he have to comment on everything?

"You sure? You took a pretty good spill."

"Is she hurt?" Odelia interjected, with a voice that was quavering, but really loud. If she'd had a stroke, it certainly hadn't affected her volume.

"She fell on her backside in the chute," he said, also speaking louder than necessary. Maybe she *was* hard of hearing.

"Well, why didn't you say something, dearie?" she asked me. "I think we have one of those donut pads around here somewhere from the time my husband Solomon was kicked in the buttocks by a young bull. Go on and ask Mama Miriam where it might be, Noah."

"That's really not necessary." I held my hand up as Noah leaned forward in the chair. "Please, don't."

"Suit yourself," Odelia said with exactly the same inflection Miriam had used earlier. They must have been living together for so long they acquired the same expressions, like an old married couple. I wondered if they were sisters, but Odelia was much smaller in stature and had none of the same facial features.

"Solomon carried that donut with him everywhere he went," Odelia continued the story. "Ha!" She laughed. "Got so used to it, he'd probably been cured for weeks before he gave it up."

Solomon? Hold on. Didn't Miriam say her husband's name was Solomon? I was semi-conscious of Odelia's voice in the background, but could no longer focus on what she was saying. My stomach knotted with the dawning realization that perhaps I was not in Kansas anymore. Could Odelia and Miriam have shared a husband? Or, was the name a coincidence, and was I just paranoid about the whole polygamy thing since my run-in with Samuel Vaullie? I looked at Odelia for a few seconds, then over at Noah, who must have caught the questioning look in my eyes. He stared hard at me. Was that a warning?

Drawing his glance away from me, he asked Odelia a question I didn't hear. I was now totally obsessed by the thought that these people, including V.A., might be polygamists. No wonder she told me it was a *complicated* topic when I asked her about it before. Did that mean that Noah was one too? I studied the cut of his jaw in profile. A new spin on the Marlboro Man, that was for sure.

Conscious of not wanting them to know what I was thinking, I tried to compose my face and feign interest in what they were saying. What was taking V.A. so long? I looked over at the kitchen door.

"The clothes need just a few more minutes," V.A. said as she finally came into the room. "Then we have to get back to town for my afternoon patients."

Still stunned by the thoughts coursing through my brain, I just nodded at V.A. She sat down next to me on the couch and joined in on Noah and Odelia's conversation. After several excruciating minutes, I tugged on the robe to make sure I wasn't going to expose myself again, and popped up. "Why don't I check on our clothes. It's a small load. They have to be dry by now."

"Your jeans were still pretty damp," V.A. said.

"I'm sure they'll be fine. I wouldn't want to make you late for those appointments." I hurried out of the room.

Rushing into the kitchen, I almost bumped into Miriam, who was carrying a stack of serving dishes. "Whoa, I didn't see you there." She steadied her load.

"Sorry." I avoided her eyes. "Just getting my clothes." I continued on into the mudroom.

Closing the kitchen door, I grabbed the load out of the dryer, sorted mine from V.A.'s and threw them on, ignoring the damp spots on the jeans. After folding V.A.'s clothes, I walked back into the living room, where Miriam had joined the others. "Here you go." I handed V.A.'s stack to her, interrupting Noah in mid-sentence.

V.A. took them without acknowledgement, and said to Noah, "Go on with what you were saying."

I continued to stand.

Turning her eyes up at me, V.A. patted the spot on the couch between her and Miriam. "We still have some time. Take a seat," she commanded.

"No thanks." I had no intention of prolonging the chat. "I'd rather stand. We'll be sitting a while in the truck."

"You *are* still sore," Odelia spoke up. "Mama Miriam, do you know where that donut cushion of Solomon's got to?"

Oh boy. Back to that again. "No. No. It's okay. I don't need it." And what was with the Mama Miriam, and Ma Odelia stuff?

"I think it's in the hall closet." Miriam stood and turned to me. "You should have said something. No need to suffer if you don't have to."

"Really. I'll be fine ..." My voice trailed off as Miriam disappeared into the hall.

If nothing else, the donut cushion topic moved V.A. off the couch.

"What do you want to do with those?" I asked, nodding at the clothes I had handed to her, hoping we could just get going.

"I'll take them back to my place. I still have a dresser full of clothes here."

"And we're glad you do." Ophelia smiled up at V.A. "Makes it feel like our girl never left."

Our girl, huh? Crazy. We needed to get out of there. I walked over and slid my hand under Mr. Bumbles collar.

Odelia patted him on the head. "He's a sweet thing."

"Yes, he is." I started pulling him toward the kitchen. "Nice meeting you." I forced a smile.

Bumping along in the truck on the infamous donut, I was begrudgingly grateful that they insisted I take it. The good-byes had been quick, thank God. I could not even look at Noah. The whole thing was so disturbing.

Halfway back to town, V.A. and I had not exchanged a word, but I caught her glancing over at me a couple of times.

"There something you want to ask me?" She finally broke the silence.

V.A. was certainly direct. I took a deep breath while considering whether to put the subject out there. I had, after all, just met these people. Maybe I had misinterpreted the situation. No. All the bells in my head screamed otherwise. Darn. Why wasn't I the type who could just let it be? The situation was bizarre, but I'm from L.A., for heaven's sake, the capital of bizarre.

"I'm confused." There went my mouth. "Both your mother and Odelia said their husband's name was Solomon."

"And?" V.A. looked over at me.

Wow. She wasn't going to make this easy. "Were they the same man?"

"Yeah." V.A. rested her right wrist on the steering wheel.

"So, you're polygamists."

"No. They belong to a religious group with a history of polygamy, and whose membership is dying out. I do not."

"I don't understand. You were raised by them, right?"

"It's called free choice." V.A. glanced over at me and back at the road.

"But," I hesitated, while picking my words. "I thought the men who head polygamist cults, by claiming to speak for God, don't allow the women and children any choice."

"Most operate that way. But my parents' group didn't, and my daddy certainly didn't."

Was she defending polygamy? I closed my eyes and traced my finger over my brow. "So, you're saying the women of your mother and Odelia's group were not brainwashed at all, that they and the children had the autonomy to leave if they wanted."

"I did, and so did my brothers."

"Were there a lot of you?"

"My mom had four kids. Odelia didn't have any of her own."

"How about the rest of your ..." I wanted to say, "weird little tribe," but I left it at, "group? How many free will polygamists are left?" Oops. I let my sarcasm slip on that one.

V.A. sighed. "Like I said, hardly any, and they're all older. They don't make the papers, because they live quiet lives."

Wait. That all sounded Hallmark card rosy, but we were still talking about polygamy. "If there's nothing wrong with your folk's form of polygamy, why didn't you stay?"

"Do I seem like the type who would want to be tied down to any man?"

"No." I smiled for the first time.

"We don't expect outsiders to understand my folk's choice of religion, but mankind has been cohabitating every-which-way since the beginning of time. They didn't corner the market on non-traditional relationships."

I guess she could be right on that last point, but there was no way she would ever convince me that anything about a cult that oppressed women and children was a good thing. Glancing over at her, I wrestled with asking another question that had been eating at me. Why it was eating at me, I don't know. It was really no concern of mine.

"Yes?" she asked. "Is there something else?"

Glancing out the back window of the truck, pretending to check on Mr. B so I wouldn't have to look her in the eye, I casually asked, "Is Noah a polygamist?"

"No, Missy. He doesn't have a dozen wives hidden at his ranch. Not even a one. So, that line you'd be standing in is a mighty long one."

When I snapped my head back around to look at her, she was wearing a half-grin. Damn. Why couldn't I keep my mouth shut? "Oh, no, no. You have the wrong idea. It's just that, you know, since you seem to know him so well, I thought maybe he shared your family's beliefs." Jeez, that even sounded lame to me.

"Right." V.A.'s eyes twinkled.

Fortunately, we reached town and she changed the subject. "Do you want me to drop you somewhere?"

"The market would be great." Still feeling unsettled about the polygamy issue, I added, "I really think someone needs to do something about Samuel Vaullie. The abuse he's inflicting on the young girls in his life is criminal."

"You want to tackle that one, Missy, you go right on ahead." V.A. pulled up in front of the market. "But make sure you have an army behind you."

"No. Wait. I didn't mean that I ..." I opened the door.

"Thanks for your help today," V.A. cut me off.

"No problem." I bent over to pick up the donut, which had fallen to the ground, and tossed it back onto the seat.

"No problem," I said again under my breath, after I lifted Mr. Bumbles from the truck and rubbed my tailbone. Better. Maybe Solomon had the right idea about the donut.

CHAPTER EIGHT

When I returned to the RV, I stashed my groceries away in the cupboard and fridge. The little store didn't have much, but I was still stuffed from Miriam's lunch. I just concentrated on the essentials, which I surprisingly never seem to have difficulty finding–Fritos, orange marmalade, almond butter, bread, bananas, and more Fritos. Toss in some yogurt and I'm good.

Walking back into the bedroom to change out of my still-damp jeans, there was Alice sprawled out on the bed. She hadn't been out of the RV in days, and I decided that after I tracked down Cal about the parts, I would somehow take her on a walk. That ought to be good. I had a leash for her that I bought when getting ready for the trip, but hadn't tried out yet. Too chicken. Alice could get really nasty if you tried to restrain her, but she needed some exercise, and letting her out in Cal's yard with the coonhounds was not a good plan. She might rip them to shreds.

I found Cal kicking back in the shade of his garage on a torn upholstered auto bench seat. Where the rest of the jalopy was, God only knew. He was draining the last drops of a can of beer when I walked up. "Any news?" I asked.

"Yep. Got a hold of 'em this morning." He set the can on the dirt next to his foot.

"And?"

"Parts will be here on Friday."

"Three more days," I groaned. "I thought I told you to have them overnighted."

Cal looked up at me and squinted. "It's fast as they could get 'em here. No sense whining about it. With the age of that vehicle of yours, you oughta be grateful they found them parts at all."

"I'm not whining." Why did talking with Cal always feel like a playground argument? Taking a moment to accept that I'd have to be in Harmony three more days, I said, "I guess getting out of here by Friday won't be so bad."

Sighing, he shook his head at me as if I had lost mine. "I said that's when the parts are gettin' here. I do have to put 'em in, ya know."

"And how long do you think that will take?" I bit my cheek, bracing myself for the answer.

"Well." He stood up and placed the heel of his shoe on the beer can. "If the parts get here by midday, I can get her started on Friday, then pick it up again on Monday." Pressing down with his foot, he smashed the can. "Should have her done by Tuesday mornin' or so."

"Tuesday morning?" I gritted my teeth. I swear to God, I could have screamed. "Why can't you work on it over the weekend?"

"Huntin'." He bent over to pick up the disk that had been a can.

"Hunting?" Was that what he said?

"Yep."

Oh God. Was I ever going to see the last of this guy? "Fine then." I stared him down. I knew I stood no chance of talking him out of huntin'. Maybe he would somehow finish the repair work on Monday morning. Right.

Getting the leash on Alice was tough. Getting her to walk with it was proving impossible. She kept shaking her head and clawing at it, trying to work it loose, but I was determined she would at least go a few feet. Half dragging her out of Cal's yard, I backed my way on to Main Street. When I turned around, I noticed Luke on the opposite side of the street, head down, walking toward town. Probably on his way to the diner, I guessed. I gave a split-second thought to crossing over to talk with him, but then felt Alice squirming like a fish on a hook, and decided we had gone far enough for the first try. Like there was ever going to be a second try. I worried a bit about that huge flapping sack of fur that hung from her belly, but if she'd rather lie around like Jabba the Hut, so be it. Alice did what whatever Alice wanted to do.

Giving up on the leash, I picked her up and was starting back into the yard when I heard some shouting from the street. It was coming from a black Honda Civic that had pulled up alongside Luke. Through the open window of the driver's side, I recognized one of the Bailey boys. Great! They just kept seeping up like pus from an infected wound.

Luke picked up speed, but they kept pace with him. I couldn't hear what they were shouting, but I knew it couldn't be good. Hugging Alice to my side, I dashed across the street and around the back of the car to the passenger side. Both the front and rear windows were down, and the other Bailey twin and a friend were leaning out taunting Luke. As I trotted up, puffing with exertion, I heard the friend say, "Hey, we're talking to you, Luuuke. Where's that slut sister of yours? She's got a fine ass."

"I bet her pussy's even better," the Bailey twin called out while making an obscene gesture. "You tell her that if she's really nice to us, we'll fuck her like we heard she likes it."

"That's enough!" I shouted at the Bailey twin. The car was still moving, but slowly enough I was able to keep up.

"This ain't your business, bitch, unless you're looking for a fuck too. You're old, but I suppose we'd do you for a price. What do you say, Jason? You wanna do this bitch?"

"I don't know. Her box is probably pretty shriveled," Jason snickered.

With my pulse pounding against my temples and my teeth clenched with rage, I lunged at Jason, who was closest to me, intending to slap the smirk off his face, completely forgetting that Alice was still in my hands. Reacting to my tensed body, she tore her front paws loose, snarled and clawed at the closest object at hand, Jason's arm. "Ouch!" he cried, reaching up to bat Alice away, but she was too quick for him. With one final slash at his hand, she twisted out of my grasp and darted up the street.

Focused on catching Alice, I turned my back to the car. As I ran after Luke, who was already in pursuit of her, I heard a final shout from the Bailey twin. "We're not through with you, bitch!" he threatened, as they sped away.

"Thanks for catching her." I looked down on Luke, who was sitting cross-legged in front of the bank holding Alice in one hand and stroking her with the other. On his young legs, he had reached her long before me, and from the way she was purring, had calmed her down, a rare feat in Alice's case. "I think you've made a friend. Alice doesn't take to many people."

"Alice?" He didn't look up.

"Yeah. Kind of a funny name for a cat, I guess."

"No. I like it," he said, more to himself than me.

I squatted down so I could see his face. "I'm Sydney."

"Yeah, I know. You were in the diner."

"Oh. You remember me?"

"Yeah. I remember everyone." He kept his eyes focused on Alice.

"Those boys were in the diner that night."

"They are not nice. Not nice. And, they are very messy."

"You got that right. They made a huge mess of my RV. Painted graffiti all over it."

"What's an RV?"

"A motorhome. You know, like people take camping."

"Yeah. Yeah. I know motorhomes. Homes on wheels. With engines. I'm going to Alaska in a motorhome."

"Really?"

"Yeah. To study the Aurora Borealis."

Wow. I wasn't expecting that one. There must have been a whole lot more to Luke than his demeanor indicated. "I've always wanted to see that." I reached out to scratch Alice behind the ear. "But we don't get them in L.A."

"Dori says we are moving to L.A. On my motorhome trip to Alaska, I will take Highway 5 from L.A. to Canada, then the Al/Can Highway to Alaska, then the Parks Highway to Fairbanks. Can I see your motorhome?"

"Sure." Shifting my weight, I decided I better stand up before my knees locked in place. I had never been a great squatter. Couldn't do somersaults either, which was a popularity killer in kindergarten. As I stood up, I noticed Dori bicycling toward us.

"What's going on here?" she asked as she stopped the bike and rested one foot on the ground.

"Alice got away from me," I said, nodding toward the cat, "and Luke chased her down. I haven't seen her this content to sit in a lap, ever."

"Yeah, animals really like him." Dori pulled her long dark hair back over her shoulder. "It would be great if we could have a pet, but we can't afford one."

"Sydney said I could see her motorhome." Luke lifted his head and looked past Dori to the street. "I'm going to Alaska in a motorhome."

"Yes, I know, Luke," she said, then turned to me. "He's been psyched over the idea of driving to Alaska in a motorhome since he was really young."

"He's welcome to see mine. It's just sitting there in Cal's yard, but it's not much to look at, more of your beached whale model RV."

"That's okay." Dori smiled through straight white teeth. "He'll be good with whatever it is."

"Her motorhome is messy."

"Oh?" Dori frowned.

I told her the story of what the Bailey boys had done to it and about filing a report with Deputy Crane.

"They just don't quit."

"You're right on that one." And, Dori hadn't even heard the latest. I planned to tell her, but didn't want to do it with Luke there.

"When can I visit the motorhome?" Luke asked again.

"How about tomorrow afternoon?" I responded, directing my question to Dori.

"That could work."

"Will it still be messy?" Lucas asked.

"I'm afraid so," I said, then hesitated, hatching what I thought would be a good deal for both Luke and me. "What would you think about my hiring Luke to paint over the graffiti?" I asked them both. "He could check out the RV and do me a favor at the same time."

Dori ran her finger across her lip, contemplating an answer.

"I could do that. Yeah, I could do that," Luke spoke up before Dori could respond.

"Luke doesn't have any experience painting RVs." Dori looked doubtful. "It may not look so hot when he's through."

"No worries on that one. Anything will be an improvement."

"All right then, Luke. You can paint the RV." Turning to me, she said, "What time do you want him there?"

"I have my dentist appointment in the morning, then I need to figure out how to round up some paint. How's two o'clock?"

"Two o'clock. Good. Good," Luke said.

"We need to get to work now, Lucas." Dori straightened her bike.

"Can I talk to you for a minute," I asked Dori, putting my hand on her forearm.

"Okay." She sounded suspicious, but turned to Luke. "You go on ahead. I'll be right there."

Once I had secured Alice in my grasp, I told Dori about the incident with the Bailey boys and their friend.

"Those little shitheads," she spat the words. "They just won't leave Luke alone. But, I can't keep him locked up in our place. He has to have *some* freedom."

"Do you think they might try to hurt him, I mean beyond words?"

"Sure. They do whatever they like and know they can get away with it, because they have that rich bitch Genevieve to defend them."

"Mrs. Bailey?" I asked.

"Yeah. Have you met her?"

"Not really. But, I saw her in action at the deputy's office."

"A real piece of work, isn't she?"

"Oh, yeah. But, I can't believe her diabolical little family is completely untouchable. The law's the law." I shifted Alice to the other arm, thinking she really needs to lay off the Fritos.

"No one is going to arrest those boys just for giving Luke a bad time." Dori adjusted her bike's handlebars to straighten the front tire.

"But, they've done far more than that. It sounds like they've been stealing from sheds, and *I know* they're the ones who tagged my RV."

"Yeah, but you gotta catch them, and they're small potatoes for Crane."

"This place doesn't keep him *that* busy." I looked up the street, which had all of three cars parked on it. "I plan on stopping by his office tomorrow after my dentist appointment."

"Well, good luck with that." She settled on her bike seat. "For someone who's just passing through, you're sure amped up about the local crap." She cocked her head at me, turned and began to peddle away.

"Well, I just ..." I sputtered to her back, then looked down at Alice. "I'm doing it again, aren't I, girl. Never content to leave well enough alone. What is it with my having to fix everything? I really need to line up a shrink when I get to New York."

CHAPTER NINE

Running my tongue over my front teeth, I was relieved to be able to open my mouth without feeling like I was auditioning for a part in Lil' Abner. As chips go, V.A. said mine was minor, but I was still impressed with the job she did. I was also impressed that when I asked her where I could buy paint for the RV, she not only gave me directions to the feed and hardware store located on the highway a few miles south of town, but also told me I could use her truck to get there. Mayberry didn't have anything on Harmony.

I decided to talk to Deputy Crane about the Bailey boys before I set off. Perhaps I was more amped up about their behavior than I should be, as Dori implied, but a heavy dose of rationalization won the argument for doing my best to see that the brats got what was coming to them. I also thought about talking to him again about Samuel Vaullie, but decided that from the education I was getting on polygamy, it was too convoluted an issue for me to tackle.

The deputy was bent over his desk riffling through a stack of papers when I walked in. At the sound of the door, he looked up over the top of his glasses, which had slid down to the end of his nose. Pushing them back up, he said, "Morning, Miss Roberts. What can I do for you?" Then gestured to the chair in front of his desk.

"I'm here to follow up about the Bailey boys." I perched on the edge of the seat. "And please call me Sydney."

"Okay, Sydney." He straightened the papers in front of him and hesitated a beat before he spoke. "Realistically, without any hard evidence they hit your RV, there's probably not much that's going to come of this. You pretty much have to catch taggers in the act if you're going to have any luck prosecuting them."

"Great," I sighed, and leaned back. "But what about the stealing they were in here for the other day? And what about the cruel way they harass Lucas Hunt." I leaned forward again and tapped my index finger on the desk. "And what about their being mean little criminals who seem to get away with whatever they like?"

"Whoa." He put his hands up and spread his long fingers. "You might want to take it down a notch or two. I'm on your side."

"Sorry, deputy." I took a deep breath and felt the heat in my cheeks as it dawned on me that my last jab had been directed at him. "I'm just so frustrated. They deserve to be strung up by their thumbs, especially for their treatment of Luke."

"I know. And, I'm on it. But my best chance for nabbing them is for theft. They're no doubt the ones who've been pilfering from garages and sheds in the area. It's just a matter of time before they slip up." He tipped his chair back. "Trust me, I'm good at my job. Justice will be served. And, it's Patrick."

"Well, Patrick." I smiled. "I'm just sorry I'm not going to be around when you serve up that justice."

"So am I." He concentrated on the papers in front of him.

"Okay." I popped up out of my chair, feeling suddenly awkward. "I'm leaving by Monday or Tuesday. If you do happen to catch them before then, would you let me know? I'll be in Cal's junkyard, pacing the fence line."

His brown eyes brightened behind his glasses. "Sure," he said and went back to his papers.

Was he flirting with me? I wondered as I walked out the door. Nah.

Driving down the highway in V.A.'s old truck, I was pretty damned pleased with myself. The shocks had probably worn out about the time the Bee Gees' voices dropped an octave, but bumping along with my elbow out the window, I felt like if I threw some bales of hay in the back you couldn't tell me from the locals. Right. Wait. What is it about a truck that makes everyone think they're cowboys?

Pulling into the gravel parking lot, I nosed into a space next to a truck that was at least as worn-in as V.A.'s. The place seemed pretty busy for being so far from the nearest town. The faded sign painted over the gaping barn-like door read Brewster's Feed and Grain. It said nothing about hardware, but it had to be the right place.

Dipping into the cavernous softly lit space, I immediately thought of my dad. Hardware stores were his sanctuary. He would actually stop at the threshold, take a deep breath, and if there had been any holy water around, I know he would have anointed himself before entering.

He would have loved Brewster's. It contained row upon row of every type of tool and gadget known to man, some of them so dusty they had to have been on the shelves since the grand opening. But the thing he would have loved the most was the smell–soft pine shavings and musky loam, mixed with a hint of acrid metal–his idea of heaven. It wouldn't surprise me if he had found his own hardware store in which to spend eternity. I don't know how my mom would feel about that, because the shelves of her heavenly hangout are probably stocked with a lot more shoes than hammers. Oh well, maybe they meet up for dinner.

As I was making my way along the aisles trying to spot the paint, I noticed that beyond the shelving was an open second level with several rounders of clothing, most of them of the denim and plaid variety. They had the same allure as V.A.'s truck. I had to remind myself that, no, three days in Harmony did not qualify me to buy bootcut jeans, and there was not a thing on those racks that was appropriate attire for the streets of New York. Darn.

After studying the paint cans, I settled on one that promised to work on metal. Even if the white was not a perfect match, I really didn't care. I just needed the obscenities covered up before I got back on the Interstate. As I was standing in line to pay, I realized that the woman in front of me was wearing one of those pioneer dresses like Ruthie's, and she had a familiar long brown and silver braid that reached to her waist. It had to be the woman I saw at the door to Samuel's house, who he referred to as Mother Helen. I was surprised he had given her a furlough from prison, but took it as an opportunity to find out how Ruthie was doing.

"Uh, excuse me," I said softly.

No response.

"Excuse me," I said, a little louder, juggling the basket of paint over to my purse arm and tapping her gently on the shoulder.

Turning her head around, she focused her close-set eyes on me, then widened them in recognition. Hardening her face, she turned back around without responding.

"Excuse me," I said even louder to her back, "I was just wondering how Ruthie is feeling."

She had made it to the front of the line at that point and used it as an excuse to continue to ignore me. That made me mad, and mad generally displaces my rational brain with one of a rattlesnake that has been rudely awakened from a nap. Setting my basket on the long wooden counter next to her, I waited until the clerk took her money, then said to the side of her head, "How is Ruthie? Is her tooth any better?"

The clerk glanced over at me when he finished counting out her change. I shrugged my shoulders and nodded my head in Helen's direction.

Maintaining a neutral expression, the clerk shifted his eyes back to her, then focused his attention on the little girl who was running up to her. It was Angela, and when she noticed me she started to lift her hand in greeting. Helen slapped it down. I gasped at the swiftness and cruelty of her reaction. "Oh my God. What's the matter with you people?" I said to her back. She reacted by grabbing Angela's arm and pulling her toward the opening to the lumberyard at the back of the building.

A backlit figure strode toward Helen, picking up speed when he saw that she was rushing to him. After a quick exchange, he turned his head in my direction and started to move toward me. Helen reached out and put her hand on his arm. He hesitated, slowly turned back toward the lumberyard, and marched out of the store with Helen and Angela trailing. It was Samuel, of course. No mistaking that brutish body language.

The clerk had lost his neutral expression, and was now staring at me with open interest. "Great people, huh," I said, nodding toward the back of the store.

"You don't want to mess with them." He pulled my paint cans out of the basket.

"Oh, I don't know, with the way they treat their children, somebody needs to mess with them," I said vehemently enough to have him halt his task.

You really do need to be alert when you drive. I know that. I have this scary habit, however, of driving for miles without being conscious of the road and whether I remembered to stop, signal, or maintain a speed that was anywhere near the posted limit. Due to my absorption in my latest meeting with Samuel and family, this was one of those times.

While my mind was off in la-la land, I hit a very deep rut. As a result, I was once again broken down on the side of the road in the hot Utah desert, this time with a flat tire. I had found the jack, located the spare under the bed of the truck, but could not for the life of me figure out how to work the damn thing loose. And the biggest nightmare, even worse than having damaged V.A.'s truck? The only person I could think of to call for help was Cal.

Desperate to avoid making that call, I decided to crawl under the truck to take another look. I was flat on my back when I heard a vehicle slow down and pull up behind me. It took less than five seconds for me to conjure up a scenario in which one of the local wackos noticed the vulnerability of my position, and decided to rape me, cut me up in small chunks, and shove me in his freezer. Why my mind always defaults to Stephen King mode rather than thinking, hey, some nice person has decided to stop and help, I don't know.

While I debated whether it was Jason or Good Sam who showed up, a pair of boots appeared at the back of the truck, followed by a knee and a hand resting on the ground. Finally, a face appeared and broke into a grin. "Taking a nap?" he asked, through an even broader grin.

Noah. Who else? What, did he moonlight as Superman? Always showing up to save the day. "No. I'm not taking a nap." I inched my way over the rough gravel. "I can't figure out how to release the spare." Finally out from under the truck, I pressed my elbow into the ground and rolled to a sitting position. Noah held out his hand, and I grabbed it and let him pull me up, but I wasn't happy about it. Yet another opportunity for me to look like an idiot in front of him.

"It's not going to happen with you lying on your back," he said, still with the smile, and now face to face with me.

"Then what do you suggest?" I let go of his hand which I had held long enough to feel his rough calluses.

"When you got the jack from behind the seat, was there a crank with it?"

"A crank? There was a metal bar thingy. I guess it could be a crank."

"If you grab the thingy." He grinned. "I'll show you how it works."

"Okay." I shrugged, stepping to the cab of the truck. His levity was really starting to bug me. I don't know what he thought was so funny.

When I handed the crank to Noah, he inserted it in a hole behind the license plate, turned it a few rotations, and the spare dropped down, just like that.

"Could they have made that any harder to find?" I asked, irritated, but feeling somewhat vindicated because I defied anyone else unfamiliar with the truck to solve that puzzle.

"A lot of trucks use this system." He set the tire upright.

"Yeah, well, I haven't had many occasions to drive a truck." He sure wasn't about to cut me any slack.

"Okay. Let's get her changed out."

"I'll handle it." I was irritated enough with him that I wasn't about to take any more favors. "I don't want to hold you up any longer."

"You know how to change a tire?"

"Sure," I said, like it was something I do every day. "My dad wouldn't allow me to get my driver's license until I understood a few basics about an engine, could check and change the oil, and change a tire."

"Wise daddy."

"Yeah, he was." I bent over to take the tire from him, but it wobbled, and the weight of it carried it right over onto the gravel.

"You ever change a truck tire before?" He bent over to help me set it back up.

"No." I stared over at the truck, thinking it was probably a ton heavier than the Jetta I bopped around in for ten years.

"Could give you some trouble."

He was right. If the lug nuts were stubborn I could be at it for hours. And what if I couldn't get the jack to work? But shoot, I just didn't want to ask for his help.

"Didn't mean to question your manhood."

"What?" I didn't get it until I saw him smile. Still with the jokes. I didn't think cowboys were supposed to be so darn jovial. With my recent track record with vehicles, I decided to concede. "You're right. I'd appreciate the help."

His response was to look back at his truck and let out a sharp whistle. I jumped, wondering what in the heck he was doing, when up bounded an Australian Shepherd dog. "Down. Stay," Noah commanded her, pointing to the shade of the truck.

"Who's that?" I asked, impressed with her obedience.

"Trudy."

"Looks smart," I said, thinking that Mr. B would definitely lose an IQ contest to her.

"She's a good dog."

Thank goodness I had the sense to have him help me, because even with the two of us, by the time we finished we were both beet red from exertion. I was definitely going to need to borrow V.A.'s shower once again. After I straightened up, I arched my back to get rid of the crick. "No Cal, yay," I said to the sky.

"What?"

"Oh, nothing. I'm just really grateful you stopped."

"I wouldn't leave you stranded." He removed his cowboy hat, combed his hair back with his fingers, and set it back on his head.

"No, I suppose you wouldn't." I studied the touch of gray in his sideburns and the strands of damp hair that curled down his neck. The neck is a highly underrated part of the male anatomy. I allowed my eyes to linger far too long on his face. Thankful that the burn from the heat of the sun masked my redness from embarrassment, I quickly busied myself with wiping the dirt from my hands. "I appreciate your help." I patted the hood of the truck. "I don't know how I can repay you."

"How about dinner tonight?"

"Oh, gosh. I'm not exactly set up for company with my RV stranded in the middle of Cal's junkyard." The guy was certainly literal.

"I wasn't asking you to make dinner for me. I was asking if you'd like to come to dinner at my place."

"Oh. Ah. You don't have to do that," I stuttered my response, his offer catching me off guard. "I've already put you out enough."

"I know I don't have to." He concentrated his eyes on me. "I want to."

Pulling away from his gaze, I glanced to the hazy horizon and back, confused by the offer and the intent. I had already read too much into my interaction with Patrick Crane that morning, and now I was imagining that there was more to Noah's invitation than dinner. My years with Harry had kept me out of the game for so long that my male gender radar had blipped out. I concluded that all this generosity I kept bumping into must be that whole Mayberry thing. He was just being neighborly. Like V.A. "Okay, that sounds nice, but I don't have any way of getting to your place, and don't know exactly where it is."

"I'll pick you up. Six o'clock okay?"

"Sure." I pushed the hair out of my eyes with the back of my hand and started around the truck. "Thanks again." I looked back.

"My pleasure." He touched his finger to the brim of his hat. Wow. I hadn't seen anyone do that since the last western I watched on Turner Classic Movies. As he walked away, he let out a sharp whistle. "Come on, girl." Trudy popped up from under the truck and followed after him.

Luke made his way around the RV with the can of paint, turning the panels into a patchwork of white on cream. I really didn't care how it turned out, so long as the graffiti was gone. If my cousin Ralph objected to it when I passed the motorhome off to him, I would look into getting a better job done in New York. I had been keeping Ralph posted about my delays, to which he expressed only marginal interest. His attention was primarily focused on the Yankees and their jockeying for a playoff berth–as it was at this time every year.

After Luke had painted over the last of the graffiti, I offered him a tour of the RV and something to drink. He was not shy about exploring every corner and cupboard, asking about the mechanics of the shower, toilet, and kitchen appliances. He even spent a few minutes in the driver's seat, humming as he checked out the gauges. He seemed determined in his intent to have an RV of his own someday.

Sitting across from me at the dinette with Alice sprawled across his lap Luke made no eye contact with me. His body language was unguarded as he shared meticulous details about his dream trip to Alaska. When he finally exhausted the topic, I broached the subject of the Bailey boys to see if I was making a bigger deal of their behavior than Luke actually felt. "What year are you starting in school, Luke?"

"Eleventh."

"Are Lloyd and Floyd Bailey in school with you?"

"Yes."

"Same grade?"

"Yes."

"What are those boys like at school? Are they popular? Do they have a lot of friends?"

Lucas shrugged and stroked Alice's head.

Oh boy, this was going nowhere. I tried a more direct approach. "How do they treat you when you're at school? Do they give you any trouble?"

He shrugged again.

"I'd like to see them rot in jail, you know, for the graffiti job they did on this thing."

That one got his attention. "Do you think that will happen?" He straightened up in his seat.

"Probably not. Deputy Crane said it's pretty hard to catch taggers."

"Oh." He dropped his shoulders.

"But he did say that there's a good chance of them being caught and prosecuted for stealing."

"What did they steal?"

"I don't know exactly. I do know that the first time I was in his office, Deputy Crane had them in for questioning about some things missing from Mrs. Anderson's shed."

"I know about that."

"You do?"

"Yes. I heard them talking about it. They think I'm stupid." He rubbed Alice from head to tail. "They think I don't understand what they're saying. But I'm not stupid."

"No, Luke, you're definitely not stupid. You're one of the brightest teenagers I've ever met." I stretched my hand out toward him, and rested it on the table.

He looked up under his dark bangs, meeting my eyes for a split second, calculating the sincerity of my words.

"What did they say?" I asked, hoping he was comfortable enough with me to open up a bit.

"They said Mrs. Anderson is old and deaf, and they were laughing about how easy it is to get into her shed."

"Did you tell this to anybody?"

"No. Dori says we need to mind our own business. We don't need other people. We just need us."

"I agree it's important for families to stick together. It's also important not to allow the Bailey twins to get away with theft, harassment, vandalism, and the other shitty things they decide to do to innocent people."

Lucas looked right at me on that comment.

"Sorry. I didn't mean to get carried away, but I have this thing about justice. It drives me crazy when the good suffer and the bad go free."

"That's not fair."

"No, it's not."

Lost in thought for a minute, while giving Alice a petting that was going to have her packing her bags and leaving me forever, Lucas finally spoke up. "They asked me if I wanted to hang out with them tomorrow night. They told me they were going on a mission, and if I helped them I could be a part of their gang."

"What did you tell them?"

"I told them, no. I don't want to be with them. I don't like them."

"How did they react when you said no?"

"Floyd got close to me. Too close to me. He held my shirt." Lucas grabbed the front of his t-shirt and twisted it. "He said *no* wasn't a good answer. He said he was going to ask me again tomorrow. He said he was going to find me and ask me again. He said I should think about answering *yes*. That *yes* would be the best answer for me and for Dori."

"Lucas, it's okay." I patted my palm on the table, but didn't go so far as to reach out and pat him. Clearly that was not a line one should cross with him, even with the best of intentions. "You don't have to do what they say."

"No. I don't have to do what they say." He let go of his shirt. Alice hopped up on the table, worked herself into a Cleopatra pose and began licking her chest. Luke scratched her behind the ears.

"What do you think their mission is?" I asked, not wanting to upset him further, but also not wanting to let an opportunity to trap the Bailey boys slip away.

He shrugged.

"Mrs. Anderson's shed?"

"Yeah. I guess."

"Deputy Crane has been looking for a chance to catch them in the act. This sounds like a good one. Would you be willing to tell him what you heard?"

"I don't know. I have to talk to Dori."

"Sure. I understand. Would you mind if I talk to her too; explain things to her?"

"I guess not." He shrugged.

"Okay, then. I'll probably stop by the diner." I scooted out of the dinette.

Luke slid out too. I had to grab Alice to keep her from following him out the door. "You've made a friend," I said, pulling her close to me as she squirmed in my arms. "She just might follow you all the way to Alaska."

Having no trouble making eye contact with Alice, he smiled, then turned and started to weave his way through Cal's rust maze.

"Thanks for your help today," I called after him.

No response. Luke's mind was already fully engaged in something else.

I caught Dori before the dinner rush, which in Harmony was probably all of four tables. At first, she wasn't keen on the idea of Luke talking to Deputy Crane. The thought of the Bailey boys having to face the consequences of their actions, however, was too much to resist. The only caveat was that Crane had to meet them at my RV. She didn't want to chance Floyd and Lloyd seeing Luke entering his office. We set it up for nine the next morning, guaranteeing that the boys would never notice a thing. They undoubtedly set their watches by western vampire time.

I made my next stop at the sheriff's office to tell Patrick what I had learned from Luke. He was a little taken aback that I had arranged a meeting without consulting him first. Given that it might help him stop the Bailey boys' wannabe mafioso crime spree, however, he was appreciative of the lead. He agreed to meet Lucas and Dori the next morning at my RV.

My last stop on Main Street was V.A.'s. She had been a good sport about the flat tire. I wrote a check for the replacement tire right away, wanting to be sure that I wasn't putting the whole Mayberry hospitality thing at risk. She was, after all, the keeper of the shower, a luxury that could not be too highly prized. By the time I reached her place, I hadn't left myself much time to get ready for dinner with Noah. Oh well, since it wasn't a *date* date it didn't need an hour and a half's worth of *date* date preparation. My plain late-to-work look would have to do.

CHAPTER TEN

I had been given the assignment of clipping some basil leaves from Noah's garden. It didn't sound like a difficult task, at least for someone who could actually distinguish a basil plant from all the other herbs he was growing. That was not I. Shoot. Why hadn't I paid more attention when my mother made her pasta sauce? Probably because eating was far more interesting to me than cooking. I decided that my best bet was to sniff a few different plants and choose the one that smelled the most like a pizza parlor.

I walked over with my cuttings to where Noah was stoking coals in a grill that was large enough to barbeque an entire cow. He told me to take them into the kitchen and rinse them off. Yay, I was right. Those thousands of pepperoni and olive pizza slices (hold the anchovies) had paid off in more than just the extra padding on my butt.

Making my way across the deep back porch, I walked through the laundry room and into the kitchen. Noah was certainly an orderly cowboy. I looked around at the neatly stacked cups, dishes, and serving pieces on open wooden shelving. It wasn't a large kitchen, but it was efficient. The appliances were all within a few steps of each other, and an upholstered banquette was tucked away in the corner under a window that overlooked a sage-brush-filled pasture.

"You doing okay?" Noah asked as he walked into the kitchen to pick up the plate of steaks.

"Sure." I patted the basil dry with a paper towel.

"There's a basket of tomatoes I picked earlier today on the washing machine." He started back out the door. "Choose some of the heirlooms and cut them up for the salad, would ya."

Oh great. I passed the basil test, but heirloom tomatoes? Looking down at his dog Trudy, who had been keeping me company on her cushion by the banquette, I asked, "Don't all tomatoes pretty much look the same?"

She cocked her head, listening, but wasn't any help.

"Oh, my goodness." It turned out the heirlooms were pretty easy to distinguish. The majority of them were not even red. I had chosen the plump gold ones, and was now in food ecstasy. If I had been alone, I would have moaned with pleasure.

"Pretty good, huh?"

"Where have these been all my life? I had no idea tomatoes could be this good. Problem is I'm guessing they'll be a little hard to find in New York."

"Not really. New York has plenty of farmers' markets."

"And how do you know that?"

"I spent some time on the East Coast looking into cattle breeds raised primarily in New England. Took a side trip to New York."

"Did you like the city?" I asked, thinking that Noah didn't seem the type to venture too far from his ranch.

"Sure. Loved the museums. Haven't you been?"

"Just once, when I was young."

"And you're moving there?" He cocked his head.

"Yeah."

"Hmm."

There seemed to be a touch of judgment in that "hmm" which kind of irked me. Watching Noah slice into his steak, I said, "It was time I left L.A."

"Uh huh," he murmured, placing the bite in his mouth.

"I had lived there all my life."

He nodded his head, still chewing.

"I need a change." Why did I feel like I had to explain everything? Why had I never learned the value of brevity? Dropping the subject, I took my own bite and looked out at the horizon. We were dining at a small table on Noah's front porch, which had been turned so we could both enjoy the view. The panorama was breathtaking in its scope. Treeless, the distant rust and chalk-colored mesas towered up into the fading blue sky. It was the first time since my being sidetracked in the area that I conceded a bit of beauty to this unique geological slice of earth. "Do you own all this?" I gestured with my chin to the endless acreage beyond the porch.

"A fair piece, with my folks."

"They live here?" I wondered why I hadn't noticed any trace of them.

"The home where I grew up is on the other side of the ranch, but my parents don't come out that much anymore. They bought a place in a retirement development in St.

George, and discovered that city life is a whole lot easier on the body than raising cattle, fun even. They're so busy with swing dancing and bus trips to Branson, I hardly see them." Noah smiled.

I smiled back, imagining Noah's mother and father swing dancing in cowboy boots.

Setting his knife and fork on his plate, he relaxed his smile, interlaced his tanned hands, and asked, "What about your folks? From the way you referred to your daddy earlier today, I'm guessing he passed on."

Noah certainly tackled a topic head on. "Yeah." I nodded my head.

"Mama too?"

"Yes. They both died pretty young." I set my fork down and looked back out at the horizon. I hadn't called my father Daddy since I was a little girl, and my mother had never been Mama, but those names simply spoken by Noah constricted my chest. It was several seconds before I could look back at him. When I did, his serious eyes were still resting on me, but he said nothing further, just went back to his steak.

We finished out the meal over the usual small talk. Turns out he graduated from Cal Poly with a degree in agriculture. Not a surprise. It was obvious he was a bright guy. I also learned he had a married sister who lived in Germany. Picking up his plates, he stood and suggested that after we clear the table we take advantage of what was left of the sunlight. He wanted to show me some of the ranch.

After visiting the chicken coop, which could have earned a four-star rating for cleanliness and amenities, we headed for a stand of cottonwood trees off in the distance. Strolling along next to Noah in the thickening dusk, with Trudy trotting several paces ahead of us, I became highly conscious of his presence. Focusing on my footing, I worked hard to convince myself that he was just an acquaintance, a stranger really, showing me the sights, like some chamber of commerce tour guide. Yeah right, a tour guide with far more than his fair share of good looks and testosterone. After spending the last five years with passionless Harry, Noah's appeal was hard to ignore.

Jeez. What was the matter with me? That was entirely unfair to Harry. How shallow could I be?

"This gorge is a favorite spot for the cattle. The only problem is they have an easy time finding their way in, but with their tiny brains, they sometimes have a tough time finding their way out," Noah said as he stopped walking. "I have to make a sweep of it every day or two."

"Oh?" I came back to the present, suddenly conscious we were standing on the edge of a steep drop-off. "Oh." I took a step back.

"Don't like heights?"

"Not really. In L.A., I made sure I either worked in a low-rise or had my desk far from the window. I always get the feeling I'm going to throw myself off. What is that anyway? It's not like I'm suicidal. I've never really looked into it? Is that vertigo?" Whew, there I was again with the too much information thing. Just nervous. But about the gorge or Noah?

Turning one corner of his mouth up in a grin, Noah stepped back with me. "I think it's a common sensation, and you're definitely not suicidal. Too spirited."

"You mean like a horse?" I frowned.

"Sure." His eyes twinkled.

"Thanks."

"It's a compliment. You have a lot of spunk."

"Oh great. Now I'm spunky."

Noah laughed. "That's a good thing."

"How can you make that judgment?" I challenged. "You barely know me."

"You left the only home you've ever known." He counted off with his fingers. "You're traveling across the country alone. From what I heard tell, even though you're only in town for a few days, you've got your back up about some of the goings-on around here."

"That's only because the goings-on, as you call them, are reprehensible." I crossed my arms. "And who told you my back is up?" Wow. Not even a local, and they were gossiping about me anyway.

"Just talk."

At least the turn in conversation had put the kibosh on any romantic notion I was having about Noah. Now I was just mad. Mad, and anxious to leave. "Well, I don't know who's talking or why, but I'm not that interesting." I turned and took a step in the direction we had come.

Feeling fingers gently wrap around my upper arm, I looked over my shoulder. Noah was standing very close. Moving around to face me, but never letting go of my arm, he said, "No. You're interesting." Then he smiled, lowered his head, and softly touched his lips to mine.

Okay, so maybe the romantic notions had only taken a split-second leave. Wow. That kiss was nice. It must have been that musk thing again. And shave cream. Definitely shave cream. I studied his face.

"Do you always kiss with your eyes open?" he asked, still standing inches away.

"When I'm caught off guard. Yeah." I turned up one corner of my mouth. "What was that about?"

"Something I've been wanting to do since you walked into V.A.'s office."

"With my baseball cap and broken tooth?" I frowned at him. "You didn't even look my way, except to watch when V.A. put me on the spot."

"No. I was looking."

I smiled, perplexed, and shook my head.

He bent in to kiss me again, and this time I closed my eyes and allowed myself to melt into the moment. With his hand on the small of my back, he pressed me so close I wasn't sure if it was his heartbeat or mine I felt pulsing between us.

When the kiss ended, I looked into his eyes. They had lost their smile, but smoldered with promises that awakened every nerve ending in my body. Willing my conscious mind to take control, I stepped back, released myself from his grasp and turned my attention to the last streak of light to the west. Okay? Where did that random moment fit in with the rest of my life? Just another Harmony conundrum, I guess.

"Well, that was fun." I looked over at him.

"Yeah." He smiled. "Although I may have chosen another word for it."

"Shouldn't we be getting back while we can still see?" I asked.

"Sure." He whistled for Trudy, then placed his hand on my shoulder and guided me to the path that led to the ranch house.

The intimacy we just shared and the near darkness in which we walked provided a shroud of privacy that emboldened me to broach the subject of Noah's polygamous neighbors. Not a romantic topic, I know, but I felt it may be my only chance, and Noah seemed to be more than well acquainted with them all.

"Would you mind helping me understand the whole polygamy thing?" I asked as we neared the house.

"You sure know how to kill a mood." He stopped to face me.

"I know the question gives you ammunition for the theory that I have my back up about the goings on around here, but put yourself in my shoes. You just don't find people like Miriam and Odelia, and Samuel and Ruthie roaming around Southern California, even as kooky as it is. And frankly, it's disturbing."

Noah brushed at the dirt path with the toe of his boot. "What do you want to know?"

"About Miriam and Odelia and V.A. for starters. They do seem strong and independent, not the type to be brainwashed by a cult. The little I know about polygamy, though, suggests it's criminally oppressive to women. It condemns them to a life of servitude to their husbands."

"I guess you'd have to ask those three women if they see it that way." Noah walked over to the steps, sat down on the top one and stretched his legs out in front of him, his silhouette backlit by the light emanating from within the house. Trudy lay down beside him, and he scratched her behind the ear.

"V.A. told me that she and her siblings always understood they had a choice, and none of them chose to become polygamists. But, I have a hard time believing they're not a rare exception." I joined him on the steps, settling down a few feet away with my back against a post.

"You're probably right about that. I haven't been keeping tabs, but I don't think there are many members of their group left."

"The thought of Miriam and Odelia choosing to share good old jumpsuit-clad Solomon is a puzzle."

Noah smiled. "Not one we're going to solve."

"Maybe not, but Samuel Vaullie is a whole other story. You'll never convince me that Ruthie wasn't forced to marry him."

"And I wouldn't try. The children in Samuel's compound are abused prisoners of a sick mind."

"If you feel that way, why has he gotten away with it? The last time I checked, child abuse is illegal in this country."

"It's complicated."

"Oh my God. That's exactly the view that V.A. and Deputy Crane take." I slipped into shoot-the-messenger mode, which wasn't fair to Noah. "Okay, I get that taking action against Samuel isn't going to be easy," I lowered the pitch of my voice, "but, these are innocent children, and there's nothing complicated about their needing someone from the outside to intercede for them."

"The only thing I can tell you is there are people who are aware, concerned, and working on it." He slid across the steps, closing the distance between us, then combed the curls off my face with the gentle stroke of his fingers. "Now, where were we?" He pulled me to him, kissed my temple and moved to my neck.

Oh boy, there's nothing like warm lips moving across the curve of my neck to ignite a fire all the way to my toes.

CHAPTER ELEVEN

In that twilight space between consciousness and sleep, my muddled mind couldn't understand why someone was hammering on the RV. Then it hit me. I looked over at the clock. Eight forty-five! Oh, my gosh! Grabbing my jeans and shirt from the floor, I quickly threw them on and flew to the door.

Standing at the bottom of the steps was Deputy Crane, dressed in uniform and sunglasses.

"Morning," I managed to croak out as I held the door open. "Come on in."

After he squeezed his tall frame by me, he slipped his sunglasses off and stood waiting in the tiny space for further instructions.

"Please, have a seat." I motioned to the dinette table.

Once settled in, he fixed his eyes on my hair in undisguised curiosity.

My hand flew to my head, and as I patted my hair I could tell it was in its usual morning shape–squished to my scalp on one side and all poufed out on the other. Great. "Overslept. Would you give me a minute?"

"Sure." His eyes smiled.

"Be back in a sec," I mumbled, as I felt my face get hot. Hurrying into my mini bathroom, I grabbed a hair band, did my best to contain the curls, ran my toothbrush over my teeth then dashed back out.

"Can I make you a cup of coffee?" I asked, taking a step toward the counter.

"I'm good. Already had two cups."

"Dori and Luke should be here any minute." I slipped into the dinette across from him.

"I'm a bit early. Habit."

"No worries." I shrugged, my mind drifting off. I probably would have been asleep no matter what time he showed up. I hadn't slept that deeply in ages. Noah's fault. We had made out like sixteen-year-olds, from the porch to the house to his truck to my doorstep.

"Any luck on getting the RV fixed," Deputy Crane was asking.

"Huh? Oh." I turned my attention back to him. "The parts are supposed to be here tomorrow. Cal said he'd have it done by Monday or so."

"Wednesday it is then." He smiled.

"You know him too, huh?"

"Oh, yeah. The good news is he's an excellent mechanic."

"That's reassuring, deputy." I smiled.

"Patrick."

"Patrick." Looking through the screen door, Dori and Luke were nowhere to be seen. Never one to pass on an opportunity to mind someone else's business, I said, "So your hobby is cold cases?"

"Yeah. They've fascinated me since I was a kid."

"Not because of TV?"

"No. You may be surprised to learn that cold cases are not solved exactly as depicted on television."

"Really?" I smiled.

"Yeah, really. There's a whole lot more to it than DNA evidence."

"Such as?"

"Searching through mountains of paperwork, mostly, looking for that one scrap that's going to give you the break you need. Sorting through dozens of witness statements, hoping to reach someone who holds a key piece of evidence he may not even realize is vital to solving the case."

"Are you working on anything in particular right now," I asked, sliding back out of the dinette. "I'm going to make myself some tea and grab a muffin. You want one."

"Sure."

"Anyway ..." I opened the cupboard over the stove and removed the package of muffins, "do you have any ongoing investigations?"

"Yeah."

"Any here in Harmony?" I asked, thinking that not a hell of a lot could happen in Harmony, except perhaps some cattle rustling.

After hesitating a few seconds, he said. "Yeah, one."

"Really? What's the case?"

"Missing persons."

"Persons–like more than one?"

"Yeah," he answered.

"Who?"

"Two young women."

"How long ago did they disappear?" I set a plate of four muffins down on the table.

"One about five years ago. The other about seven."

"Any leads?" I started to ask, just as Dori and Luke appeared at the door, cutting off the topic.

"Hi. Good to see you." I pulled the screen door open.

Patrick stood up to greet them, but I could tell he immediately sensed that his uniform was making Luke nervous. He turned the passenger seat in the cab around and perched himself in as casual a pose as he could muster with his thin legs bent up to his torso. Uncle George's RV was definitely not suited for hosting dinner parties or pow wows.

After saying hello, I motioned for Luke and Dori to sit down at the dinette on the side facing Patrick and encouraged them to have a muffin. I also brought a pitcher of orange juice, and glasses to the table.

Alice came out of the bedroom, arched her back and immediately made her way to Luke's lap. Thank you, Alice. She may be a cranky sort, but on occasion she does come through. Luke immediately started stroking her back.

Not wanting to overwhelm Luke with an extra presence in what was a challenging situation for him, I excused myself, grabbed my muffin and cup of tea and moved to the bedroom. I was well within hearing range, mind you, as I still had a vested interest in the Bailey boys.

After Luke told Patrick verbatim about the boys' plans for the evening and their demand that he take part, I heard Patrick say in a low even tone, "I know those boys have been bothering you for a very long time now, Lucas, and tonight we have an opportunity to change that, but only if you want to. No one would think any less of you if you chose not to participate. I don't want you to do anything that makes you frightened or uneasy."

I heard Luke talking to Dori at that point. She responded in reassuring tones, then after a long pause, Luke said with conviction, "I will do it. Yes. Yes. I will do it."

"Okay then, Lucas, we have some plans to make," Patrick said.

"Plans. Good. I like that."

When I heard the sound of the screen door opening, I stepped out of the bedroom and grabbed Alice before she seized the opportunity to follow Luke out the door. Touching my free hand to Dori's forearm, I asked, "Are you okay with this?"

"Okay as I *can* be." She flipped one side of her long black hair over her shoulder. "I think Luke can do this thing, and we could use a bit of redemption in our lives right now, both of us."

"Okay, good." I pulled my hand away and propped Alice up with it. Holding her was kind of like trying to carry a twenty-pound bag of sand.

"One thing, though." She bore her eyes into me. "I have to work tonight, so I won't be there. That means you need to be. Luke is fairly calm with you, and you need to have his back if things go sideways. Crane will have his hands full with the other boys."

"Sure. Of course." I looked over at Patrick, wondering how he felt about taking someone along on his stakeout.

"Good then. Bring Luke to me the minute it's over," she said to both of us.

We nodded in agreement.

After they left, Patrick stayed behind to catch me up on the plans. Luke was to let the Bailey boys know he had changed his mind about going with them to Mrs. Anderson's. He was also to tell his sister the hour they were meeting so she could pass the information along to Patrick.

We were sitting in Patrick's personal vehicle, a non-descript, square, blue sedan–standard equipment for the detective trade, apparently. It was tucked around the corner away from Mrs. Anderson's house, but with a side view to both her front and back yards. The Bailey boys had told Lucas to meet them behind her house at ten. It was nine forty-five.

To kill time, I decided to pick back up on Patrick's cold case hobby. "Can you tell me a little bit about that missing persons case you mentioned this morning? How old were the girls?" I asked.

"Early teens."

"You said one disappeared about five years ago, and the other seven?"

"Yeah."

"Seems like that would have been big news."

"You would think so." He tapped his fingers on the steering wheel. "But, the parents of the girls never reported them missing. Officially, there's no case."

"What? That's crazy. What makes you think they're even gone?"

"Shortly after I moved here, a witness to their disappearance found out about my investigations. She asked me to look into it."

"Wait. Let's back up. So, your witness has evidence the girls disappeared, but no one, including the parents, reported them missing?"

"Basically."

"I don't understand. Who were these girls?"

"They lived in Samuel Vaullie's compound."

"Of course," I sighed. "I should have guessed. So, who's your witness?"

"I'm not free to say."

"But, she's credible?"

"Oh, yeah."

"Good luck getting anything out of Samuel and company. According to the whole darn town, they're pretty much untouchable."

"I don't know about that." He turned his head toward me. "There's always a way."

"Now wait, so you're saying you're going after Samuel? According to talk around here, law enforcement doesn't want to have anything to do with polygamists. They implied you're no help at all."

"And it's fine by me if they keep thinking that."

Not the reaction I was expecting. "Hmm, any solid leads?"

"One name keeps coming up."

"You gonna to tell me who it is?"

"What do *you* think?"

"That would be a no?"

"That would definitely be a no."

"I'd love nothing more than to see that bastard Samuel put away for life," I said, thinking that with Patrick's analytical mind and patience, he might just pull it off. "I may have to leave my address in New York with you, so you can let me know where to send my poison-pen letters to him."

Patrick's attention was suddenly drawn to a point over my shoulder, he said, "Here we go."

I turned to look out the side window of the car. In the distance, through the moonlight, I could just make out a dark figure standing next to Mrs. Anderson's tool shed. "Luke?" I asked.

"Probably. He's by himself."

A few minutes later, three hunch-shouldered figures strolled up to him.

We watched, expecting them to break into the shed, as that was their previous target, however, they started toward the back of the house instead. Luke, lagging just behind, hesitated, and turned his head in our direction. Patrick had told him where our car would be parked. One of the boys must have said something to him, because he turned back to the group, picked up speed and followed them to the house.

"Now what?" I asked.

"I need to trail them. Wait here." Patrick grabbed the door handle.

"Really?" I frowned at him.

"I don't want to chance their seeing our movement."

"Got it."

He had already turned the interior lights off in the car, and he left the door open slightly to avoid making any sound.

After three long minutes, I slid across the seat and exited the driver's side door, leaving it slightly ajar as Patrick had done. Ducking down and keeping a low profile, I moved to a scrubby bush just off the gravel road that would offer me some cover. It gave me a direct shot of the back of the house.

It was not my intention to interfere with Patrick's work, but I'm definitely not the *wait in the car* type. No. I'm more of the *dig through every closet until you find your birthday surprise* type.

Patrick was about halfway up the slight knoll on which the house rested, but near the corner of the house farthest from me, out of the boys' peripheral range.

While the others stood and watched, one of them moved from window to window, testing the locks. When he hit pay dirt, he gestured for the others to move closer. Sliding the sash up, he pulled the screen out, and set it on the ground. A split second later and in one quick motion, three of the boys grabbed the fourth and forced him through the window. From the way he was struggling, it had to be Luke. Poor guy. This was more than he had signed up for.

One of them let out a quick laugh, which caused the leader to grab him by the arm and get in his face. After looking around to see if anyone had heard, one by one they pulled themselves over the sill and into the house.

Looking over at Patrick, I watched him move toward the window, his body bent in half. He didn't attempt to go inside, however. Instead, he sat down with his back against the wall to wait.

I sat down also, crossing my legs, and entwining my fingers, wondering how on earth I was going to explain this all to Dori. Luke had to be scared to death. I was surprised he hadn't just blown the whole thing by yelling for help.

Patrick told me he had chosen not to tell Mrs. Anderson about the sting, thinking it may cause her to deviate from her normal routine. But breaking into her house moved the criminal activity to a new level. And Luke was involved. Damn.

We waited and waited. Then finally, a lone figure emerged from the window. It had to be Luke. After hopping to the ground, he turned his head toward Patrick, who must have whispered something to him. Then he knelt down so they were head to head. After less than a minute, he ran directly toward the car where I was supposedly waiting. Oops.

I popped up and scooted toward the car so I would beat Luke there.

"Oh, my gosh, am I ever glad to see you," I whispered loudly when he joined me, wanting to hug him. I pointed toward the far side of the car instead. "We better move to where we can't be seen." After we crouched down, using the car as a shield, I asked, "What happened in there?"

"They pushed me through the window."

"I know. I'm sorry. How'd you get away from them?"

"When I fell to the floor, I crawled to the couch and squeezed behind it. I didn't make any noise."

"Good for you. What did they do when they discovered you weren't there?"

"They whispered my name, and then they said I was gonna pay."

"Don't worry about that, Luke. You're not the one who's going to pay. They are." I moved to my knees, as my legs were starting to tingle. "How'd you get out without them seeing you?"

"When they left the room, I waited, and then I crawled back out the window."

"Good thinking." I patted his shoulder.

He shrugged my hand off.

Hearing a commotion coming from the house, I whispered, "Stay behind the car, Luke. I don't want them to see you."

He nodded and sat down, his back against the door, seeming more than okay to remain out of sight.

As I moved around the front grill, I was just in time to see Patrick grab one of the boys as he climbed out of the house. Pulling his hands behind his back, he handcuffed his wrists together. The next one out of the window, who was carrying a large bag, put up a tougher fight. While Patrick was wrestling with him, the third boy leapt out the window and started running toward the front of the house.

Damn it. That little shit was *not* going to get away. I tore across the yard. When I reached the front, I pulled up, panting hard and shifting my weight off my tender ankle. Watching him head for the open field on the far side of the house, I sighed, exasperated.

Just then the sound of a rifle shot exploded through the night air. Holy shit! My heart about jumped through my scalp. I looked over at the movement on the front porch. Standing there was a diminutive old lady in her full-length nightgown, holding a rifle about as tall as she was. Quickly looking back toward the boy, I noticed he had bent down and wrapped his arms over his head for cover.

Shouting, "Don't shoot me!" to the old lady, I seized the chance and took off once again. The boy uncovered his head, just in time to see me dive for him and knock him over.

What was I thinking? Underneath me, he was fighting like a cat in a bathtub, clawing and pounding at whatever he could reach. But, I was too angry to let him win the match. That was until he bit my forearm.

"Ouch!" I yelped as he shoved me aside. "God damn you!" I grabbed for his ankle as he started to stand, but I missed.

He was two steps into his escape when I heard a quavering but loud voice say, "You stop right there, young man."

He had no intention of doing that, until he glanced over his shoulder to see little Mrs. Anderson with her rifle pointed straight at his head.

"Whoa, lady, take it easy." He started inching away, his eyes locked on hers. "I wasn't doing nothing."

What an idiot. It was either Floyd or Lloyd. It didn't matter. They're interchangeable. "Listen, you moron, you've got a gun pointed at you. Do you really want to keep running?"

He hesitated, while the question tried to penetrate his tiny brain.

Mrs. Anderson waggled the tip of the rifle for emphasis. I liked this lady, although I was a tad uneasy about her skills as a marksman.

"What's it gonna be?" I looked at Floyd/Lloyd then nodded at Annie Oakley Anderson for emphasis.

"You really want to die tonight, Lloyd?" It was Patrick's voice coming up behind me. I looked up over my shoulder. He was prodding the other two handcuffed boys with his nightstick, while toting the bag I had seen one of them carry out of the house.

"She's not gonna shoot me." Still with the belligerent attitude, even with a gun pointing at his head. Wow.

"You want to test that theory?" asked Patrick.

"Huh?" he asked.

"Just give it up. Don't make a bad situation worse. You run now and, first of all, you're going to be caught. Second, the judge will go a whole lot harder on you."

The guy was just not that smart. His tensed muscles signaled he was about to take flight again, but this time he was not going to get away. Still on the ground, I had moved within reach, and when he started to bolt I grabbed both of his legs and he fell flat on his ass.

By that time, the rookie deputy from Patrick's office had arrived. Thank God. I was not cut out for police work. I noticed for the first time the blood oozing from the bite on my arm.

Standing up, I glared down at Lloyd and raised my forearm. "Look what you did to me, you little punk. Have you been tested for rabies?"

"What I did to you, bitch? You knocked me down, and she shot at me." He rubbed the back of his head and jutted his chin toward Mrs. Anderson. "My mom's gonna sue you both."

I sucked in my breath through my teeth. "She can just go right on ahead and do that," I said as the rookie grabbed him by the arm and roughly helped him to his feet. "You can hear all about it from your jail cell. Do you know what the other inmates think about spoiled brats like you?" I moved within inches of his face. "They have them for breakfast."

"You're nuts, lady!" He sneered at me, although his attitude had lost some of its edge.

Guiding Mrs. Anderson to the house while gently removing the rifle from her hands, I overheard Patrick ask her if she was all right. When she nodded in the affirmative, he made plans to return the following morning to talk with her.

Next, he helped the rookie put the boys into his cruiser, then headed toward the sedan. I walked over to join him. Luke was exactly where I had left him.

"Are you okay, Lucas?" Patrick asked, shifting the bag to his left hand and offering his right hand to help him up.

Ignoring it, Luke pressed his hands to the gravel and stood up on his own. "Yes. I'm okay."

"So, what did they steal?" I nodded at the bag.

"Looks like some silver, but also an antique revolver," Patrick replied.

"Wow."

"Yeah. Really stupid on their part."

"So, what happens to the boys now?" I pressed the hem of my t-shirt into my bleeding arm.

"I'll talk with Mrs. Anderson in the morning, and also get a warrant to search their houses. I finally have good grounds to look into whatever other illegal activities they've been up to. How bad's the bite?" Patrick nodded at my arm.

"He broke the skin. Do you think I should I be worried about an infection?"

"I don't know. Maybe."

"V.A. mentioned a doc in town, but wasn't too keen on him. Do you think I ought to see him?"

He hesitated before he spoke. "You're probably better off stopping by V.A.'s to let her take a look at it."

"A doctor that no one uses–another one of the many quirks about this town. How does the guy stay in business?"

"Good question."

"It's kinda late to be knocking on V.A.'s door. And I have to get Luke back." I turned my head toward Luke, who was looking more than ready to go.

"She won't mind. She's not much of a sleeper."

"And how do you know that?"

"Her lights are on all hours of the night." Patrick smiled. "I'll drop you and Luke at Dusty's. Are you okay with walking back to V.A.'s from there?"

"Sure."

Patrick was right about V.A. She was up and more than happy to help me with my arm, although typical of V.A., she was underwhelmed by my injury. Her remedy was to run it under water for a long time, apply a good dose of antibiotic ointment and tell me to keep an eye on it.

CHAPTER TWELVE

The next day, walking into town, I felt the best I had since I left Los Angeles. Mr. Bumbles seemed to be in a good mood too, his tags jingling as he trotted along smiling and casting his huge brown bloodshot eyes up at me.

Yes. We were finally making progress on putting Harmony behind us. Cal had gotten word that the parts were to arrive that afternoon, and he even said that he would try and get some work done on the RV when they arrived–*try* being the operative word with Cal.

The other thing that had me bouncing down the street with Mr. B was that Patrick had called my cellphone to say that when he searched the Bailey boys' room, he found my Sandy Koufax bobblehead doll and my Dodger cap. Woo Hoo! Uncle George would be very happy. And the best news of all– the Bobbsey Twins were going down!

Patrick was seated behind his desk filling out paperwork when I walked in.

"Hey, Patrick. Okay to bring him in?" I asked, nodding at Mr. B.

"Oh sure." He set his pen down.

I took the chair opposite the desk, and Mr. B plopped down beside me.

"So, you had some success with your warrant."

"Yes. In addition to your things, I found several items Mrs. Anderson listed as missing. That, combined with catching the boys coming out of the house with a bag full of her stuff, makes it a pretty tight case."

"Where are they being held?"

"They're not. They've been released."

"Already?"

"Oh yeah, their mother had them out in a hot second."

"Of course. She isn't about to let her babies suffer the consequences of their actions."

"No. Not likely."

"Do you think a court will give them any jail time at all?"

"Maybe some. They did steal a gun." Patrick picked his pen back up and tapped it on his desk. "But the jails and prisons are so full now, it's more likely they'll end up with probation and community service."

"Well, I wish them many miserable hours on their hands and knees cleaning public toilets with toothbrushes."

Patrick laughed, reached down under his desk, and handed me a paper grocery bag.

I opened it and pulled out the bobblehead and Dodger cap. Upon close inspection, they looked in good shape. "Yay! Thanks for your help with this." I held up the loose-necked Sandy Koufax.

"No problem. Just don't let it get around that I aided a Dodger fan." He smiled.

"It'll be our secret." I smiled back.

Tapping his pen more rapidly on his desk and not looking me directly in the eye, Patrick said, "It's Friday."

"Yeah." I sensed an awkward moment coming my way.

"Buffalo steak night at Dusty's."

"Oh, that's right." I tried not to concentrate on his Adam's apple. "Dusty did mention that."

"Feel like going?"

Was that an invitation? "Sure. I guess," I reached down to pat Mr. B. He was always a good diversionary device for smoothing over awkward situations.

"Great. I'll tell Dusty to plan on two more steaks and meet you there at six."

"Okay." I was really confused. Was he inviting me to dinner or drumming up business for Dusty? The men in that town were sure hard to read. But, what did it matter, anyway? In a few days, all seventeen-hundred-plus people in Harmony were going to be a wacky fading dream. Thank you, Lord.

Late that afternoon, V.A. was once again generous enough to let me use her bathroom to get cleaned up for Dusty's barbeque. To celebrate my farewell to Harmony, I decided to break out one of my rarely donned dresses and apply a little makeup. The dress was a simple brown one, a bit farther above the knees than it would have been on someone shorter. My legs were the one feature on my bod I actually felt pretty good about, even if they were a mile long. I checked my backside to make sure that there were no hidden surprises. What the heck, if Harmony didn't approve, it was no matter. I was never going to see those people again anyway.

When I walked into the living room, V.A. was straightening the magazines on the end table by the couch. As she stood up, a look of surprise crossed her face. "You *do* know that it's just a barbeque, right, Missy?"

My face reddened immediately, of course. So much for my not caring what other people thought about my clothing choice. "Yes. I do."

"You got a date?"

Jeez, V.A. was direct. "No," I said a little too quickly and loudly.

"Well, okay." She walked over to her desk, apparently through with that line of questioning.

"I appreciate the use of the bathroom. It would have been an awful week without it."

"For all of us." She let out a loud laugh at her own joke.

Smiling at how pleased V.A. seemed with herself, and shifting my bag of dirty clothes to my shoulder, I said, "I need to get these to the motorhome before I head to Dusty's."

"I'll give you a lift."

"You don't have to do that."

"I'm heading out to pick up Ma Odelia and Mama Miriam anyway." She pulled open her top desk drawer and grabbed a set of keys.

"Sure then. Thanks."

On the short ride, I decided to relay the story of the Bailey boys' arrest. Naturally, V.A. had already heard it. Why I thought the news wouldn't have already spread to the entire population of Harmony, I don't know. In the ensuing silence, I broached the subject of Patrick's missing persons' case, certain that V.A. would know all about it also. I had been wondering what she, with her polygamy connections, thought about it.

"Patrick told me about the case that he's working on regarding the missing Mormon girls."

"Alleged missing."

"You don't believe the story?"

"I didn't say that." She took her eyes off the road to look over at me. "It's just that in all this time there's been no evidence come to light that anything happened to them."

"But, according to Patrick, who heard it from a reliable witness, no one has seen them in years."

"That's not unusual, though. There are a lot of children out there that no one outside their group has ever laid eyes on."

"That's just not right."

"And why do you think that?" she asked, obviously well aware of the answer, but for some reason wanting to hear it from me.

"Because if Samuel Vaullie is an abuser as I suspect, he can do virtually anything he wants to them. He can molest them, bend their minds to his will, and there's no one to protect them."

"Uh huh," V.A. nodded her head, deep in thought. Studying the set of her jaw as she focused on the road once again, I got the sense that she was far more interested in the case than she let on. That made me feel better about the situation. If she set her mind to it, maybe V.A. could be a big help to Patrick.

As I made my way up Main Street to Dusty's, I studied the shadows on the illusory mineral-laced mesas in the distance. At that time of the evening, between the unforgiving over-bright day and the ebony night, it was easy to understand why artists and photographers so loved the high desert.

Yes artists, not you, I reminded myself. You don't like the desert at all. Remember? Looking back down at the road, I almost gasped in surprise at the number of cars and trucks lining both sides of the street in front of Dusty's. It was the first time there was evidence of more than a handful of people living in the area.

Following the strains of a George Strait tune through the door–no modern country for this crowd–I made my way through the crush around the counter and scanned the room for Patrick. I finally spotted a long arm waving me over to the horseshoe shaped corner booth.

As I approached, I saw he wasn't alone. V.A. and her mothers–*so weird*–were squeezed in next to him. Funny V.A. hadn't mentioned it on the ride. Well, that was going to be awkward.

"Hey, everyone." I forced a smile as I stood dumbly at the end of the table. What made it even more uncomfortable was that Ma Odelia was cocking her head, running her eyes up and down my dress.

"Have you met Mama Miriam and Ma Odelia?" Patrick asked, acting as host.

"Yes. Nice to see you again." I nodded at the women.

"How's your tailbone?" Ma Odelia practically shouted. Apparently her hearing aids had not adjusted to the noise from the diner crowd.

"Fine." I looked over at the next booth and checked to see who may have heard about the condition of my butt. Fortunately, they were busy talking.

Still standing, I wondered how I was going to fit into the booth.

"On Friday nights, it's communal eating around this place," V.A. said, reading my mind. "Pull up that chair behind you there. I'll clear some room." She shoved condiments to the middle of the table as I scooted the chair over and sat down.

With Patrick to my left and V.A. to my right, I was having a hard time keeping my knees from being crushed between theirs. I finally moved back a bit and almost knocked into Luke, who was carrying a tray of water glasses. "Oops, sorry, Luke," I apologized, as he reached over my shoulder to set the glasses down.

"How are you doing today, Lucas?" Patrick asked.

"Good." He left quickly–a man on a mission.

"You think he really *is* doing okay after last night?" I directed my question at Patrick.

"I do. Dori and he are feeling good about Floyd, Lloyd, and Jason being pretty much confined to their houses until the court proceedings are over. I don't think even *they* are stupid enough to make it harder on themselves by continuing to harass Luke."

"Don't be too sure. Those are pretty dim bulbs."

"You're right about that," he said, smiling, "but I'll keep tabs on them."

"Good."

"Are you planning on staying in town much longer?" Mama Miriam drew my attention across the table.

"Not much. The parts for my motorhome finally came in, so I should be on my way Monday afternoon or Tuesday morning, I hope."

"Will you be happy to be out of here?"

Whoa. I guess I know where V.A. got her probing conversational style. "Well, I do need to be on my way. My cousin was expecting me in New York by now," I lied. He wasn't exactly the worrying kind, at least not about anything but his sports teams.

Interrupting our conversation, Dori, pad in hand, hurried up to the table and asked for our order, a welcome relief, as I wasn't enjoying being the main topic.

Turns out that on buffalo steak night, the order taking is not too difficult. It amounts to deciding if you'd like yours tall, grande, or venti. Oh wait, that's Starbuck's, but it's basically the same idea. The other unique twist is that you carry your own uncooked steaks to the grill. All part of the fun, according to V.A.

When it was our table's turn for the grill, V.A., Patrick, and I sidestepped our way through the crowd coming and going through the backdoor. Miriam and Odelia stayed behind, leaving V.A. in charge of their steaks.

Standing at the far side of the treeless yard was the biggest grill I had ever seen. It beat Noah's by a steer and a half. Behind it was Dusty, barely visible through a veil of smoke. He was wielding what on closer inspection turned out to be pitchfork-sized tongs in one hand and a squirt bottle in the other. At least a dozen townspeople circled the grill, apparently quite content to be bathed in spitting bison fat, smoke, and the occasional errant flame.

Following V.A.'s lead, I squeezed into the crowd on one side of the grill. When Dusty saw us standing there, he shouted through the smoke, "How do you want them cooked?" After our responses, he took our plateful of steaks and set them on different sections of the grill. Wondering about the condition of his lungs, I used Patrick and V.A.'s preoccupation with the people around them to get out of range of the smoke.

Studying a group conversing on the other side of the yard, I noticed a familiar stance and cowboy hat. Noah. The uptick of my heartbeat surprised me. What was the matter with me? I should have absolutely no interest in the guy. I was leaving. Soon.

As if he could feel me staring, Noah looked over at me and put his finger to the brim of his hat in salute. Who does that? Jeez.

I blushed, nodded my head in his direction, hoping I was too far for him to see my reaction. Moving back toward the grill, I became very interested in slabs of buffalo. Right.

A minute later, I felt a hand on my upper arm and looked over my shoulder to be met by the crystalline blue of Noah's eyes. I blushed again, of course. Damn. Why couldn't my emotions ever cooperate?

Motioning with his head and tugging on my arm, Noah indicated he wanted me to follow him away from the grill.

When we reached the fence, he pulled his hat off and wiped his forehead with his arm. "I didn't figure you for the buffalo steak night type."

"Patrick invited me." I looked over to where he and V.A. were standing, still deep in conversation with the other diners.

"That was real hospitable of him." Noah followed my glance to the group around the grill.

"What's a buffalo steak night type, anyway?" I was already annoyed and we had just started talking.

"Someone who would not necessarily be inclined to show up in a short skirt." He looked down at my legs.

"I didn't realize that a uniform was required," I felt the heat rise both on my face and in my voice. "And, it's a dress."

"A very nice dress, too." Noah set his hat back on his head, one side of his mouth still turned up in what I perceived as a mocking grin.

"Thanks." I rolled my eyes, turned away from him and looked back over to the grill to find Patrick watching us, a perplexed look on his face.

I raised my hand in a weak wave, and Noah nodded his head.

"It's a pleasure chatting with you," I said insincerely, turning back to Noah, "but I'm sure my steak is done by now."

"Well, you best not let your bison burn."

"Okaaay. I won't. Enjoy your evening."

"Thank you." Noah tipped his hat to me. "I think I'll do just that."

"Well good." I walked away, feeling Noah's eyes on my back the entire way to the grill. Whether they actually were on me, I have no idea. Nonetheless, I willed myself to put one foot in front of the other and ignore the voice in my head that condemned me for not just sticking with jeans.

V.A. and her mothers and Patrick had a fine time at dinner, hashing over Harmony news while downing a whole lot of buffalo and a tableful of sides served family style. While I actually liked the steak, my exchange with Noah left me unsettled and without much of an appetite. I was thankful my place at the table left my back to the room, because I didn't want him looking at me.

During the course of the meal, in what felt like an afterthought, the group occasionally tossed a question or comment my way. I understood, though. This wasn't my town, after all. But still, sitting there, an island unto myself, did give me that lonely, away at summer camp kind of feel. I realized I *was* lonely, but not for the home I left in L.A., for a home I had yet to establish, a life I had yet to create.

Just as we were about to dig into our dessert of strawberry shortcake and vanilla ice cream, I heard the loud clicking of heals on linoleum. A dark presence looming up on my left followed it. Genevieve Bailey. Who else in town had stilettos sharp enough and an ass hefty enough to make that sound?

"You!" She bent down until her cleavage was eye level with Patrick and drew her shocking-pink-tipped finger from its holster and stuck it right in his face. "How dare you put my sons through the trauma of being dragged into jail! And all over a trumped-up charge of stealing from daft old Mrs. Anderson."

"Floyd, Lloyd, and Jason were caught leaving her house with a bag full of her possessions, Mrs. Bailey, and you know I found some of her things in their room." Patrick's tone was as even as it had been all evening. Amazing. As low as his voice was, however, the entire diner heard, because the place had gone dead quiet with Genevieve's entry.

"Well, I just don't believe it!" She vigorously shook her head, with her breasts and bottom jiggling like molded gelatin salad at a Thanksgiving feast.

I looked over at Ma Odelia, her eyes wide and her mouth open in disbelief. V.A. and Miriam, on the other hand, were tensed and leaning forward, ready to jump right into the mix.

"There's a lot of material evidence against them, Mrs. Bailey." Patrick inched over to move out of breast range.

"So you say, but you're totally biased. You've had it out for them for years."

"I'm not going to talk to you about this anymore, Mrs. Bailey. We need to leave it for the courts."

"Oh that's right, clam up, you coward." She put both hands on the table and leaned toward him, which placed her butt right in my face. "This is going to be the end of your career in this town! My sons have done nothing wrong, and you're going to look like a fool when we prove that!"

Okay, that was it. I tapped her on the back. "Excuse me." She didn't respond, so I tried again, a little louder, "Excuse me!"

Genevieve pushed herself away from the table, twisted around, and glared down at me. "What?"

Standing up to give myself the height advantage, I was now looking down at her, my fists pressed into my sides. "*What*, lady, is that you are rude and you are wrong. I don't know why the hell you think it's okay to march in here and ruin our dinner like some raving mad queen of the castle. Your sons are delinquents. You're delusional. And, you need to leave this table now before our ice cream melts!" Why I added that last bit, I don't know, except I do hate melted ice cream.

"Who are you?" She sneered up at me.

"I'm one of your precious little sons' victims, and I'm this close to filing another criminal complaint against them." I unclenched my fists, squeezed my thumb and index finger together and gestured in her face.

She slapped my hand away, stunning me with her viciousness. Wow! I held my breath before reacting. Thank God for the counting-to-ten lesson my father had drilled into me. Not that it worked very often, but this was one crazy woman, and I wasn't about to engage in a catfight with her. A catfight? Exactly when had my life disintegrated to the point that I was thinking in terms of a catfight? I really needed to get out of that town.

"All right, ladies. No need to go at each other like this." It was Noah, who had walked over while I was preoccupied with the witch woman. He placed his hand on Genevieve's back, and drew her attention away from me with the concerned expression in his eyes. "You don't want to spoil folks' evening, now do you, Genevieve? It's Friday night, after all. Why don't you walk on over to the counter with me, and I'll buy you a drink?"

With his touch, her body transformed from poised for a fight to taut for action of the sexual kind. Straightening her back so that her boobs were positioned like twin atomic missiles ready for launch, she tilted her head, stuck her bottom lip out, and pouted, "Oh all right, Noah, if you insist. I couldn't stand another moment with these vile people anyway."

Leaving his hand on her back, he guided her away from the table, taking a split second to look back at me and wink. Wink! Like this was some kind of horseplay. And what was with him intimating that *I* was going at *her!* Ugh!

When I turned back to my tablemates, the quartet was staring up at me with their mouths open. I sat back down on my chair.

"Well, Missy," V.A. said, breaking the silence, "that's the most excitement we've had on buffalo steak night since Abe Vincent choked on a French fry. Ha!" Nodding at my strawberry shortcake, she asked, "Has your ice cream melted?"

I stuck my spoon into the dessert and looked back up at the group. They were all suppressing grins. I grinned back and started to laugh. "I believe it's still edible."

"Well, that's a relief." Miriam joined in my laughter, relaxed back into the booth, and the mood at the table lightened considerably.

The mystery of whether or not Patrick had invited me as his date was solved with the arrival of the check. He split that thing five ways down to the penny, including the tip. It was a relief, really. It had been a little bit nuts on my part to think that Patrick had anything else in mind. He was too much of a facts man, and the fact was I–was leaving town. No use wasting time and money on me.

As our group was breaking up, I stole a glance at the counter to see if Noah and Genevieve were still there. They were. With the diversion of Miriam helping Odelia position her walker, there was a good chance of my leaving without being spotted.

And I had almost succeeded, when Dori stopped me. "Sydney. Can I talk to you for a sec," she asked, tucking her order pad into her apron, "outside?"

"Sure, I guess." I glanced over her shoulder to check on Noah. Fortunately, Genevieve's back was to me, but Noah was sitting sideways to the counter, and although seemingly engaged in conversation with the witch, he glanced over at me. Ignoring his gaze, I followed Dori and the rest of my group out the door.

After exchanging good-byes with the Loomis women, I thanked Patrick for including me in the evening, politely skipping over the part where it had almost turned into a brawl.

Dori gestured for me to follow her to the corner of the building. "I'm having a meeting tonight at my house, and I want you to come." She cast her eyes down the street then back at me.

"Oh? What kind of meeting?"

"There's a group of us who support women and children who either have escaped from, or are trying to escape from, the polygamist brutes who control them. We're meeting tonight, and I'd like you to be there."

"But, why me? I'm only here for a few more days."

"Look, this meeting is specifically about Samuel Vaullie. I've heard the tone in your voice when you talk about him. You need to be there."

"Need is a pretty strong word," I said, warning bells clanging in my head, "and, I still don't see what I could possibly do to help you."

"You have something else going on tonight?" Dori put one hand on her waist.

"Well, no."

"Then, just come."

Looking off in the distance, I thought there was absolutely no doubt I was going to live to regret it, but I of course said, "All right," as my sales resistance is nil. My cupboards in L.A. were the place where infomercial bargains went to die.

"Good. I'm getting off work early. The group is meeting at nine. We live above the garage behind the beige house with the porch, just a ways beyond Cal's place." Dori threw her hair over her shoulder and rushed back through the door before I had a chance to change my mind.

I started to head back to my little oasis in Cal's junkyard, when I heard Noah call my name. I hesitated and turned back, half-expecting to see Genevieve draped all over him. She wasn't.

"You going home?" he asked, as he reached me.

"Yeah. If you can call it that." I looked down the street toward Cal's.

"I'll walk you."

"What's the matter, you lose your girlfriend?" I looked back at him, rolling my eyes. It was snarky of me, but I couldn't help it.

"No. She's still inside, working on her fourth bourbon." One side of his mouth turned up, and he started to grin. *So irritating.* "And you know she's not my girlfriend."

"Do I? There's a hell of a lot more I *don't* know about you than I *do*." Why was I even engaging in this kind of talk with the guy? I needed to shut up and stop acting like I cared.

"We can change that." He straightened the hat on his head. God, he was tempting.

"Not a lot of time to do that." I pulled my eyes away from his.

"So, why waste it? Let me walk you home."

"I'm good." I turned to head back down the street, wanting to distance myself from those damn pheromones of his that sucked me in like pet hair to a vacuum cleaner.

"Now wait a minute." He reached out and gently encircled my forearm with his calloused hand. "It's a nice evening. And, I don't imagine you have anything better to do."

"But, I do."

"Oh, really? And what might that be?"

"I agreed to attend a meeting at Dori's house."

"Oh?"

"Yes." I stepped back, so that he let go of my arm.

"One of Dori's anti-polygamy meetings?"

"Yes."

"So, you *are* involved."

"No. It's not that. It's just that Dori and Luke have had a rough go, and I wanted to be supportive."

"Well, you best watch out, because if I know Dori she'll be looking for much more than support."

"No need to worry about me in that regard, because I'm not going to be here past Tuesday."

"So, you've said." He smiled again, like the fricking Cheshire cat. Jeez.

"I'm going to go now." I gestured toward Cal's.

"Okay, but I'll take an IOU on that walk tomorrow morning, only we'll make it a hike. You haven't seen any of Zion Park yet, right?"

"No, but…"

"But, what?" He cut me off. "You can't possibly have something to do tomorrow too. It's Harmony. It's Saturday, and as you keep telling me, you're just passing through."

I looked past his chin to the hair curling down his neck. It was no use. He could make a fortune selling those pheromones. "Okay, what time?"

"I'll pick you up at nine."

"Nine it is." I turned to leave. "See you then." I started down the street.

"Yes, you will. Oh, and I wouldn't object to your wearing that dress again," he called after me.

I halted mid-step, but didn't turn around, suddenly conscious of my hem riding up my thighs. Raising my right hand, I fluttered my fingers at him. I was never going to wear that dress again.

CHAPTER THIRTEEN

My walk to Dori's apartment was a dark one. I guess there's not much of a budget for streetlamps in Harmony. The keychain flashlight, that Harry insisted I carry, finally came in handy as I used it to guide myself around the house and several cars to Dori's above-the-garage apartment. A simple sconce hung to the left of her front door, barely lighting the stairs and landing.

Dori answered my knock right away, opening the door to a scene that was a marked contrast to the murky soup I had just waded through. The small space vibrated with color and life, a reflection of Dori's decorating style, which mirrored her wardrobe, an amalgam of retro hippie, earthy native and bold modern.

Cushions, metal card table chairs, and a narrow bench were scattered against deep turquoise walls and occupied by women of varying ages and looks, whose easy chatter conveyed familiarity. So caught up were they in their conversations they barely glanced in my direction when Dori led me to the bench, a refreshing relief after the curious stares I had been receiving all week.

She offered a quick introduction to the woman who scooted over to make room for me. Her name was Francis Rush, and the soft gray streaks at her temples and creases around her eyes made me think that she was somewhere around fifty. We had just exchanged hellos when Dori settled onto a floor cushion, and crossed her legs. "Okay, everyone, we'd better get started. We have a lot to cover tonight. First, this is Sydney Roberts." She nodded in my direction. So much for my anonymity. "She's had some dealings with Samuel and has met Ruthie. At the last meeting we talked about needing to involve more people from outside, so I asked her to come tonight."

I raised my hand in hello. Their return looks were far more open and receptive than I thought they would be, considering they knew nothing about me.

Wasting no time, Dori looked over at the young blonde woman on the cushion next to hers, and continued, "Sarah, how are things going in Salt Lake?"

"Phillip has enough help now that they can make the rounds of the streets most days and nights," Sarah answered, looking down at notes on a loose sheet of binder paper. "He's also made progress with the shelter and counseling help, thanks to many of you." She acknowledged them with a glance around the room. "But the whole job thing is another story. There's still just not a lot out there. And straight out of their groups, without the means to support themselves, you know how vulnerable they are. They can be talked into using the shelter, but it's so disorienting for them. If they have any chance of making it, they need a place they feel is a safe haven."

Confused from the outset, I whispered to Francis, "Who's she talking about?"

"Women and young people who either escape from or are thrown out of their groups," she whispered back. "Without any place to go, many of them end up on the streets of our bigger cities."

A discussion ensued regarding different people and agencies they could contact for help with job prospects, as well as funding for training. After several of the women divvied up the responsibility of calling potential leads, Francis initiated the next topic. "Marie made contact with me again. She still has a lot of fear about leaving, but I think she's getting closer. Her attitude has changed a lot since they banned Edward. It was such a heartbreaker for her on top of losing Christine."

"You think she's strong enough?" another young blonde sitting on a chair across the room from us asked.

"I do," Francis answered. "Her tolerance for watching her daughters being plucked away from her one by one and handed over to their uncles and cousins is waning. I think she is finally angry."

"It's about time," Dori spoke up.

"Agreed. I don't think it's going to take much more than a nudge, but we need to be prepared for her if she's going to go through with it," Francis said. "I'll continue to watch for opportunities to talk to her, and call the committee if she decides to make her move before the next meeting."

Okay. I told myself not to get drawn in. Just sit there, fulfill my obligation to Dori and hightail it back to the RV. But, the whole *not getting drawn in* thing never works for me. I'd like to think that being a sucker for causes is noble, but it's more likely due to an unhealthy desire to help–with everything. Harry says it's a control issue. Another thing to consult a shrink about. Whatever. I just couldn't keep my darn mouth shut.

"Excuse me," I said, turning to Francis. "I'm trying to follow what's being said, so do you mind if I ask a couple questions?"

"Not at all." Francis shifted so she was facing me.

"I take it that this Marie wants to leave her polygamist husband, correct?"

"Yes."

"How old is she?"

"Around forty, I think."

"Is she being held against her will? I mean, is she free to come and go?"

"Ask her husband, and he'll tell you she's a free woman, made whole and happy by fulfilling her obligations under God's law," Francis answered. "The reality? So long as she's with him, she has no will of her own. Rather, her will has been bent by the leaders of her group to align perfectly with *their* will."

"But she told you that she's unhappy and that she wants to leave?"

"Yes."

"And I take it that her husband is as miserable a man as Samuel Vaullie?"

Francis nodded her head.

"So, if she has all of you to help her," I said, looking around the room, "why doesn't she just go?"

"I'll answer that one," a woman with fiery eyes two chairs down from me spoke up. "Leaving comes at a dear price, so dear most women are unwilling to pay it."

At my quizzical look, she continued, "When a woman leaves a polygamist group, she leaves the only home she's ever known, and she often gives up her own children."

"She doesn't take them with her?" I asked.

"The leaders are highly unlikely to give up any of the children, particularly girls. So, a mother generally escapes with little more than the clothes on her back." She glanced at the other women. Some of them nodded in agreement. "When you encourage someone to break away from polygamy," she continued, looking back at me, "you do so with the knowledge that you're tearing her away from children or grandchildren who will be devastated by the loss. Women who escape rarely reveal the atrocities they lived through. If they do, it's likely the leaders will never again allow them contact with family they left behind. The leaders end up with few witnesses to their criminal abuse and fraud. A perfect plan."

"Women are social beings, Sydney." She held my eyes with hers. "Take our social and familial network from us, and we plunge into a very dark place."

"We?" I shuddered inside. "So you all made that choice?" I looked around the circle.

"Most of us," she answered.

"And the younger ones of us were banned." Dori drew our attention with the fire in her own eyes.

"But, if there's such a shortage of young women, why would they do that?" I asked her.

"They don't abide rebelliousness, and they absolutely won't tolerate interest in things from the outside world, from either girls or boys. Show any desire for electronics, music, makeup, or clothes one too many times, and you're out. They love banning young men, actually." Dori flipped her hair over her shoulder. "It's less competition for the older men for teenage brides."

"That's horrible." I grimaced at the too vivid picture of Samuel with Ruthie.

"Horrible for those teenage girls, yes," Francis interjected. "And that's why we're here, but in the end if we can get help for them, banishment is a blessing for the boys. Phillip, the man Sarah mentioned, was banned, but ended up making it through college, and now has a successful career as an engineer. And he's using his success to help other young men and women who show up on the streets of Salt Lake."

"Luke would have been crushed had he not been banned," Dori added. "The leaders don't have the patience for anyone who's different. They had no clue what to do with him. He was definitely no use to them."

"So, you were both banned?" I asked.

"Yeah. Been on our own ever since, and doing just fine."

"Amazing."

"We better move along," Francis spoke up after looking at her watch. "As you know, Ruthie is getting close to her due date. Has anyone seen her in the last few days?"

The women shook their heads.

"I don't imagine that Samuel is going to let her out and about at all, and we still have yet to communicate with her that she needs to call us for help if her labor becomes difficult."

"That's right, if she gets into trouble, we can't let Doc Schrum get near her, the damn quack." Dori slapped the floor.

"He'll kill her." She looked around the room. "He's done it before."

"We don't know that for sure," Sarah said quietly.

"Then what happened to Gloria and Joannie? Tell me that," Dori said.

"Let's not get into that right now," Francis spoke up before Sarah had a chance to answer. "Our immediate concern is to make sure nothing happens to Ruthie. We have to find a way to get a cellphone to her, and convince her of its necessity. Any ideas?"

The room was silent with spinning minds.

"What about V.A. Loomis?" The question spilled from my lips before I could stop it. I was doing a really great job of keeping a healthy distance from the situation. Right.

"Go on," Francis said, turning to me.

"Ruthie has been having trouble with her teeth, and I was thinking that perhaps you could talk V.A. into calling her to come into the office under the guise of her needing a follow-up."

"Wouldn't Samuel or Helen be with her?" Dori asked.

"Yes. But, maybe one of you could be waiting in the exam room when V.A. brought her in."

"I'm not sure that V.A. is the right person to ask for help on this one." Francis pressed her finger into her chin.

"Oh?" I wondered what the objection could be to what I thought was a pretty dandy idea. Then I remembered V.A.'s own polygamist background. "Oh."

"Now wait." Dori straightened her back and cupped her hands over her knees. "V.A. was raised a polygamist, but so were we."

"Yes. And her mothers would still be practicing it if her father hadn't died," Sarah spoke up.

"That wouldn't stop V.A. if she decided to start taking an interest in what's been going on with Samuel," Dori said. "It's pretty obvious she has her own mind."

"You lose nothing by asking," I said.

"How 'bout we leave that to you." Dori turned to me.

"Me?" I frowned. "You all know a lot more about the situation than I do."

"Yeah. We do," Dori said, "and V.A. may tell us the idea stinks and she won't cooperate. But then, hearing an outsider's view on the situation, she may also take a long think about what's at risk if Ruthie can't call for help if she needs it. What do you say, Francis?"

Francis intertwined her long fingers in her lap and stared at the floor for a few moments. "I suppose it wouldn't hurt to try. If V.A. turns us down, it'll give us time to come up with some other way to get to Ruthie. Though, it would be best if V.A. could somehow see Ruthie tomorrow." She looked over at me. "We don't want to risk her going into labor before we can get to her."

Oh boy. So, they elected me to talk V.A. into lying to Samuel Vaullie–V.A., who has probably never been talked into anything in her life. Why? Why? Why didn't I keep my brilliant idea to myself?

"Are you in, Syd?" Dori focused her determined dark brown eyes on me.

I inhaled and straightened my back. "Okay, I'll give it a shot."

"Good." Francis shifted on the bench and grabbed her purse from underneath it. "Call Dorcas with V.A.'s answer as soon as you can," she said to me.

Dorcas? I looked over at Dori. She scowled at me. "I will," I said, turning back to Francis.

"I think that about wraps it up for tonight." Dori stood up.

"Very nice meeting you." Francis held out her hand to me. "And thanks for agreeing to help us out."

"My pleasure." I shook her hand, looking into her eyes. As worried as I was about V.A.'s reaction to my request, I really meant it. My problems were mere inconveniences relative to what these women must have gone through to rebuild their lives.

I lagged behind the rest of the women who were leaving in order to get Dori's cellphone number.

"You can do this thing," she said as she handed me the slip of paper, like she was my coach or something.

Funny kid. As I looked at her baby smooth skin, it struck me that in L.A. she would still be hanging out in coffee houses with her friends, worrying about men and her bod, instead of pregnant fifteen-year-olds. "Thanks." I turned to leave. "You'll hear from me as soon as I know something."

"Good."

"Goodnight, Dorcas." I started down the stairs.

"Don't call me that," she grumbled, but as I looked back over my shoulder she was smiling.

On my walk back to Cal's, I was so absorbed in forming the next day's conversation with V.A. that I paid little attention to my surroundings. After a few minutes, it occurred to me that I was hearing the sound of a rough engine just behind me. I think the reason I hadn't noticed it any sooner was, in L.A. it would be strange *not* to hear the sound of an engine anytime, anyplace. As the car pulled even with me, I sped up, suddenly conscious of how dark it was and that I was the only person on the road.

"Hey bitch," a voice pierced the silence.

Great. They were back. There was no mistaking that nasal whine. And, taking on the Bailey boys at that time of the night and all alone was not a good plan. I moved even faster.

"Bitch! We're talking to you!" The car swerved slowly to move within a few feet of me.

Focusing on the light coming from Cal's yard in the distance, I continued to ignore them.

When the car moved even closer, I inched as far off the road as I could and finally looked over. One of the Floyd/Lloyds was hanging out the back window, drumming the door panel. "What's the matter, you fucking whore, not as tough without the deputy around?"

I continued to keep up my pace. "Are you guys really that stupid to risk even further legal problems by violating the terms the court set?"

It was too complicated a question for them judging from the dim-witted looks on the faces of both the twin in the driver's seat, and the one in back. "How 'bout a little payback, bitch?" The driver sneered out his window as he turned the car sharply, screeching to a stop within a foot of crushing me under his wheels.

I jumped back, ran around the rear of the car, and sprinted toward Cal's, my heart pounding with fear that the twins intended to crank up their illegal activity level from malicious mischief to felony, as in murder of a tall redhead. With their engine roaring even louder as they came after me again, and with only about a hundred feet left to the gate, I screamed into the dead night air, praying that Cal hadn't wired himself up to earphones, "Help! Help me!"

Faithful Mr. Bumbles and the coonhounds immediately started baying, delighted to take up my cause–any excuse to bark. The twins beat me to the gate, digging their tires into the gravel as they spun the car to block the entrance.

Panting hard and feeling trapped, I was considering my next move, when I heard the sound of popping and watched in confusion as Floyd and Lloyd screamed like little girls and threw their bodies down onto the seats of the car.

Squeezing himself between the gate and the hood of the car, a small rifle trained on the driver's window, Cal appeared like an angel in prison-jumpsuit orange and edged over to me. "You all right?" he asked.

"Yeah." I expelled my breath, bent over, and rested my hands on my knees. "Yeah, I'm okay."

"Well, good." He moved over to the car and stuck his gun through the window. "All right boys, sit on up."

"No," came the answer from the back seat. "Not 'til you get that gun away from us."

"What's the matter, you think I'm gonna shoot ya?"

"You did shoot at us, you crazy redneck bastard," again from the back seat.

Then from the front seat, "And we're gonna report you. Your ass is gonna be grass, dude."

"How you figure? You gonna tell the deputy you were out harassing this lady here, when you're not supposed to leave your house, huh?" Cal poked the seat. "Get on up, right now, or I *will* shoot ya."

Reluctantly the boys moved to a sitting position.

"Now, I wanna see the whites of your eyes while I talk to you boys, so you look on over here and listen up." Neither boy looked over. "I mean it, you." Cal waved the gun barrel in their faces. They reluctantly dragged their defiant eyes in his direction. "First thing, you apologize to Ms. Roberts. Look at her when you do, and mean it. Now!" He waggled his gun again.

"Sorry," they said in unison, resting their eyes on me for a split second.

"Next boys, you ain't never gonna bother her again." He ducked his head down so they were looking right at him through the window. "Because if you do, I *will* come after you. I will bring misery on your hides, and no one will ever know it was me. You got that?"

When they didn't respond, Cal said, "Nod those sorry heads of yours and show me you got that."

They nodded, heads bent, their defiance deflated with the threat.

"Okay, you go on now, straight home, and do not defy me." He tapped each one of them on the shoulder with the barrel of his gun.

After they maneuvered their car back onto the road and disappeared into the dark, I looked over at my savior, wondering if he wore that jumpsuit twenty-four seven, perhaps even over his pajamas. The only thing missing from his usual uniform were his shoes. He was barefoot. "You sure came in a hurry."

"Heard the dogs. Knew something was up." He tucked his gun under his arm.

"Well, thank you. I don't know what they might have done had you not shown up." My heart was just beginning to resume its normal pace.

"They probably wouldn't a run you over. They're nasty little pieces of work, but not of the Charles Manson sort."

"That's good to know." I studied the hair fanning up from the back of his head. "Were you asleep?"

"Just getting that way. Got an early start tomorrow. Huntin'."

"Of course, huntin'." I crossed my arms and hugged them to my chest. "Don't let me keep you."

"You gonna be all right?" He studied my face.

"Oh, sure," I said, seeing him for the first time as a man rather than a Saturday morning cartoon character. He was genuinely concerned, and I vowed to keep that in mind the next time he tested my patience. "Are you going to be able to make your way back to your garage apartment without stepping on something?" I nodded down at his feet.

"Miss, I know every inch of this place. I can find my way through the yard blindfolded." Cal turned and whistled for the hounds.

I was glad he called them, because I planned on having Mr. Bumbles sleep in the RV. On a night like this, I could use his company, and even Alice's, providing she decided to give us the time of day.

CHAPTER FOURTEEN

Waking from a dead sleep at the sound of Mr. Bumbles low woofing at the door of the RV, my pulse shot into high gear. Were the Bailey boys were back on the prowl? Then I squinted at the clock–six a.m. Nah. Couldn't be. I plopped my head back down on the pillow as my heartbeat slowed. Not their time of day, I reassured myself, but six a.m.?

"What's going on Mr. B?" I asked, as I tightened the sash around my robe, joining him at the door. Then I heard it, the unmistakable baying of Cal's coonhounds. Mr. B bounced up and down on his front legs–if you can call lifting them a half inch off the ground bouncing–and turned his hangover eyes up at me.

"Okay, let's see what's going on." I opened the door while holding on to his collar. Through the dawn haze, I could just make out the figure of Cal standing next to the cab of his truck. His pack of hounds was gathered around his feet, in full hyper-mode. Before I could stop him, Mr. B lunged away from me and headed straight for them.

Sliding into my sandals, I hurried after him, afraid that Cal might want to include Mr. B in the hunt. When I reached the truck, Cal was already in the cab. Jostling my way through the dogs, I walked to the driver's side window and motioned for him to roll it down.

"Aren't you taking the dogs?" I looked down at them and back up at Cal, whose hair had to have been combed with an eggbeater.

"Nope. Can't."

"But, I thought they were for hunting."

"Not big game. I'm going after pronghorn. The hounds would give me an unfair advantage."

"Oh, okay," I said, not really understanding. "Pronghorn?"

"You might know 'em as antelope." He started his engine. "Time's a wastin'. Gotta be on my way."

That didn't explain the whole unfair advantage thing, but did I really care? No. "Well, good luck, then." I backed away from the truck, checking to make sure I didn't trip on the dogs.

As Cal rumbled through the gate, I feared they might follow him all the way to his hunting grounds, but he poked his head out of the window, shouted an indecipherable command, and they tore past me into the bowels of the junkyard, with Mr. Bumbles taking up the rear.

Antelope? I headed back to the motorhome. And, the words and music to *Home on the Range* began spinning around my brain once again.

An hour and a half later, I was on my way to V.A.'s, certain she would be awake. If I was going to convince her to talk Samuel into bringing Ruthie by, I needed to do it face to face, and before Noah picked me up for our trip to Zion.

As I neared Dusty's, Patrick approached me from the other direction.

"You heading in for breakfast?" I asked, nodding at the door.

"Yeah. You want to join me?"

"I can't. I'm heading over to V.A.'s, but I'm glad I ran into you. The Bailey boys tracked me down last night. Scared the shit out of me, actually."

"What did they do now?" He frowned in exasperation.

"I was walking home from Dori's, and they chased me with their car. If it hadn't been for Cal, I don't know what would've happened."

"Cal?"

"Yeah. He heard my shouts, came running, and chased them away." I left out the part about the rifle. There was no need to reveal Cal's methods, in the event it may be necessary for him to use them again.

"Man." Patrick sighed deeply. "I was hoping they would keep their noses clean until they appeared before the judge."

"Too stupid."

"That's for sure. Do you want to file another complaint?"

"Not really. You have enough on them. They're not worth another second of my time."

"Do you want me to warn them about leaving you alone."

"No. Cal covered that."

"He did?"

"Yeah," I said without further explanation. "Enjoy your breakfast."

"Sure. Bye." He reached for the door handle.

V.A. answered her squeaky screen door in her lab coat, looking as if she had already been at work.

"You open every Saturday?" I asked.

"No. I work two of them a month to accommodate people who can't make weekday appointments."

"That's good of you."

She shrugged her wide shoulders. "It's my job."

Looking past her to the waiting room, I asked, "Do you mind if we sit down for a minute?"

"Okay." She sounded wary.

Choosing a chair over the couch to make sure I wasn't below her in height, I sat down. I needed all the advantage I could get. It was going to be a tough sell.

"So, what's the mystery, Missy?" V.A. set a chair at a right angle to mine.

Thinking it wouldn't serve me to dance around the topic when V.A. was a straight-to-the-point woman, I said, "I went to Dori's meeting last night after the barbeque." I knew that in Harmony there was no need to explain the nature of the meeting. I was sure V.A. would be aware of the group.

"And?" V.A. folded her hands in her lap.

"They're very concerned about Ruthie. She's so young. They want her to be able to get help if her delivery becomes difficult and, like you, they don't trust Doctor Schrum." I was proud of myself for coming up with that point, for V.A. couldn't have an argument against it."

"And?" she asked again.

Boy, the woman was not going to make this easy.

"They want to get a cellphone to her, so she can let someone on the outside know when she starts into labor. They also want to reassure her there are people who will be there for her if she needs them. As you know, Samuel has her completely cut off."

"Yes."

"So, they asked me to ask you about the possibility of having her come in for a re-check on her bad tooth. They thought there'd be an opportunity to pass her a phone in the exam room."

"They?"

"Well, we. No, actually me." I decided there was no way around full disclosure with V.A. "I was the one who proposed the idea. I remembered seeing her here for that bad tooth."

"You need to be a little more specific about the details of your clandestine operation."

"Well." I cleared my throat. "What we thought was if you could talk Samuel into bringing Ruthie here, then Francis Rush could be waiting in the exam room to talk to her and to offer her the cellphone. It'd be best if it happened sometime today. Her delivery date is very soon."

V.A. blew out her breath through her lips and stared down at the floor. Looking back up and straight into my eyes, she said, "You're asking me to bring Ruthie in here under false pretenses, to lie to Samuel."

"But is it a lie? Really? She was suffering quite a bit with that tooth."

V.A. continued to stare at me.

Oh no. I read her body language. I was losing her. "Look." I stared right back into her eyes, "I know the whole polygamy thing is supposedly complicated, but there's nothing complicated about wanting to help a young girl. She'll be in real physical danger if something goes wrong with her delivery. This is our chance to prevent that. We should at least try."

V.A. paused for several more seconds. I willed myself not to squirm under her look. I also willed myself to keep quiet and resist my usual urge to fill the silent spaces, and to let V.A. come to her own conclusion in her own time.

"Okay. I'll make the call to Samuel, but if he resists I'm not going to push it."

"Oh, good. Thank you." I released my breath. "If you're successful, Francis will be waiting for your call." Reaching into my pocket, I pulled out her number.

"You were pretty sure of my answer." She reached for the slip of paper.

"No, not really." I relaxed the muscles in my face for the first time since I entered. "I was just hoping."

"You given any thought as to why you're so invested in the situation when, as you keep saying, you're just passing through?" she asked as she stood up from her chair.

"A little, but I decided to leave it to a shrink." I smiled.

V.A. was still chuckling as I screeched through the screen door. At least I left her laughing.

Mr. Bumbles was waiting beside me at the gate when Noah pulled up precisely at nine. Cal's dogs were positioned behind us in various stages of sniffing, sleeping, and peeing, and Mr. B kept looking around to check on them.

Noticing that his dog Trudy was not in his truck, when Noah hopped down out of the cab, I said, "We're not taking the dogs?"

"No. Not this trip. The park only allows dogs on one of the trails, and it's not my favorite."

"Oh. Okay." I looked down at Mr. Bumbles, thinking that it was no loss for him. He was going to get to spend the whole day with his buddies. "Give me a minute while I make sure there's plenty of water for him. I know Cal leaves a lot around for his dogs, but I'm not sure how good they are at sharing."

"If you have a light rain jacket, you should grab it, oh, and an extra pair of socks and sneakers," Noah called after me.

"Really?" I looked up at the cloudless sky.

"Yep. We're at the tail end of monsoon season, and you don't want to get caught."

"Monsoon season?" I looked back over my shoulder.

"This is our rainy time of the year."

It is? I visualized the truckloads of dust I had been wading through for the past week.

"And don't forget a hat. You don't want to burn," he called again.

Now, a sunburn I believed, but as a redhead I never went anywhere without a cap.

After checking to see that Alice was still contentedly sprawled out on my bed, I set out Mr. B's bowl and patted him good-bye, then joined Noah in the truck.

"Zion National Park is where I was headed when the motorhome broke down." I fastened my seatbelt.

"You were a little off course, weren't you?" He looked over at me as we cruised past the smattering of buildings in town then picked up speed.

"A misinterpretation of the route I was given."

"Sounds like a fancy way of saying you got lost."

"Here's another one for you. I'm severely directionally challenged."

"I thought everyone in California made their way around by the navigation system in their high-priced cars."

"There you Utahites go again, making judgments about people from California." I frowned at him.

"Utahites?" He grinned.

"Well, what is it then?"

"Utahns."

"Okay, Utahns then. You Utahns seem to think Californians are one big mass of purse-dog-carrying techie clones, when we're not. And, by the way, have you seen what I'm driving?"

"Good point. So, given that you're directionally challenged," Noah's eyes twinkled, "can we trust you're actually going to end up in New York?"

"My cousin Ralph faxed me the directions. I have them taped to the dashboard of the RV."

"Glad to hear it. Wouldn't want you to end up lost in some small town in Nebraska. They might not be as friendly as we are."

"No. They might not." I studied his profile. Indeed not. My mind wandered to the evening I had spent at his ranch.

"Tell me about Zion," I said quickly, hoping he couldn't read my thoughts. "Do you spend much time there?"

"As much as I can, although that doesn't amount to a lot with the responsibilities of the ranch."

On the journey to the south entrance of the park, Noah told me about its history and natural features. As we drew closer, the horizon filled with stunning plateaus, which soon enveloped us, and I understood he had not over-exaggerated a thing.

"They don't allow cars on the scenic drive this time of year, so we're going to have to use the shuttle to get to our trail," he said as he pulled into a stall at the visitor's center.

Stepping down from the truck, he reached behind his seat. "I brought a backpack along for you. You can put your jacket and shoes in it."

"Okay." I opened my door, still curious about how a bright blue sky was going to produce any rain.

Feeling the heft of the backpack when he handed it to me, I said, "Whoa, what'd you pack for me, a brick?"

"No. Water. You're going to want it."

"Exactly how far are we hiking?" I asked, realizing I had failed to mention that most of my previous hiking experiences had been confined to the local high school track. That was several Januarys back–a New Year's resolution that predictably flamed out just in time for me to bury my shame in cheap Valentine's Day chocolate.

"You'll be fine." He pulled the straps of his own backpack up over his shoulders.

Yeah. But, that didn't answer the question. I placed my jacket and shoes into the main pocket of the pack.

"How's your ankle?" he asked, staring down at my feet. "Any soreness left?"

"No, not really." I turned it back and forth to demonstrate. "But, you do realize I'm not any kind of serious hiker woman, right?"

"Yeah." He smiled. "I guessed that."

"Good." I frowned. "I think."

"You're gonna love it." Moving around behind me, he adjusted my pack on my back and gave my shoulder a reassuring troop leader pat. "Let's go catch a shuttle. I want to stop at the Human History Center first, so you can see their film. It's a good overview for someone who hasn't been here before."

After the film and a quick trip around the museum, we hopped back onto the shuttle and rode it to the Temple of Sinawava stop. On the ride up, my neck couldn't swivel fast enough to take in all the craggy buttes reaching for the heavens, the light reflecting off their white caps. It was easy to understand why the early pioneers had named many of the sites in the park from the vocabulary of angels. If God were looking for a place to set up shop, this would definitely be in the running.

I was delighted to find there was a bathroom at the stop, with a flush toilet even. When it comes to using pit toilets, I have been known to dehydrate myself until my teeth stick to my lips rather than use one.

After a swig from our water bottles, we set off down the Riverside Walk, which according to Noah led to the Narrows, a part of the park he said was a favorite of photographers.

After following the river for a while, I called to Noah's back, which was twenty feet ahead of me, "Hold up a minute."

He stopped and turned. "Sorry about that. I get focused on the trail."

"I can see that." I ran my thumbs under the straps of my backpack. "Can we rest for a sec? Stop and smell the ..." I gestured toward a tree just off the trail, "Whatever these are."

"Box elder."

"So, you're a naturalist too?" I smiled at him.

"No. Not really. These are pretty common."

"I love the sound of rushing water." I looked toward the river. "Let's get a little closer." Picking my way around bushes and through the dirt, I stepped onto a boulder and stared down at the river tumbling over rocks in a low wide waterfall.

"Not much water in the Virgin right now, but that can change in an instant." Noah stepped up beside me onto the rock.

"Oh, yeah?"

"This area is known for its flash floods. See all the debris piled up against that tree." He pointed to a nearby cottonwood. "That's all from flooding. You don't want to be caught along the river, and particularly in the Narrows, during a rainstorm."

"Isn't that where you said we're going?"

"Yes. But we're just going to wade up a bit, so you can get the feel of it."

"Wade?"

"Yeah. That's why I had you bring the extra shoes and socks. You hike *in* the river."

"Okay," I said skeptically. "This is going to be a first for me."

"It's a lot of fun, particularly this time of year when it provides relief from the heat. And again, we're not going that far up. Not that I think you can't handle it." He smiled.

"That's okay." I smiled back. "I moved beyond trying to impress a date with daring physical feats at about the same time I figured out I would never be able to twirl these legs in a cartwheel." I patted the top of my thighs. Darn. Did I just refer to him as my date?

"To impress the girls in school, my specialty was skipping rocks."

"Oh, yeah. Let me see what you got." I was happy the date comment didn't seem to faze him.

Noah stepped off the boulder, bent down and fingered a few rocks before selecting one. Taking a sidearm pose, he wound up and flung it across the top of the water. It skipped five times. "Well?" He stretched out his arms and grinned, waiting for my reaction. "Are you suitably awed?"

Adjusting my baseball cap to make sure the bill was still shading my face, I said, "I give that a nine, for form and distance."

"Not a ten?"

"Nope. Need to leave room for improvement."

We continued up the trail, now walking side by side, flanked by trees and bushes bowed by a long summer's growth. The quiet intimacy of the setting created a comfortable silence between us. Per my usual, however, the silence was short lived. My overactive curiosity about what makes people tick compelled me to ask Noah, "As much as you love your ranch and this state, you ever want to live anywhere else?"

"When I was in college I became interested in water treatment implementation for developing nations. I had an opportunity to work in Africa."

"That's a leap."

"Not at all. If you're managing land and livestock, you're managing water."

"Why didn't you end up there?"

"The ranch has been in our family a very long time. My sister wasn't interested in working it, and eventually my father wasn't going to be able to handle it on his own, so that left me."

"Any regrets?"

"Not a one. You play the hand you're dealt."

"No asking for a reshuffle?" I looked over at him.

"No. No point."

"I'm not sure I could be that noble."

"No nobility involved. Living in the place I do, doing the work I do, is pure privilege."

"Wow. That's humbling. You trying to make us discontented types look bad?"

He laughed, then stopped walking, grabbed his water bottle out of his pack and took a few gulps. "So, it's discontentment that spurred this journey of yours?"

"I hadn't thought of it in those exact terms, but yeah, I guess you could say that. I don't know. I'd been in L.A. all my life, but it wasn't just a change of scenery I was looking for. It was ..." I hesitated as I looked up at the cliffs across the river, "that this inner voice kept telling me there had to be more to life than what I was living."

"The old *Wizard of Oz* syndrome." Noah put the top back on his water bottle.

"Huh?" I cocked my head at him.

"Girl runs away from her dull gray life and ventures through an emerald world for a spell, only to discover she'd rather be home, because, as it turns out, there's no place like it." Noah's eyes brightened.

"That's a tidy little analysis you came up with," I said, my ire immediately dialing up. "Naturalist, psychologist, you really missed your calling." I started back up the trail, sorry I had opened up to Noah at all, and more than ready for the hike to be over.

"Wait a minute." He gently touched my shoulder. "I was just having fun with you."

"That's the lame excuse people use when they make a joke at someone else's expense."

"All right. I deserve that. I apologize." He dropped his hand. "Now, go on. I want to hear more about this journey you've undertaken."

"Right."

"I do."

"Why?"

"Because you interest me."

"You mean like a lab rat?"

"No." He laughed. "Like a good-looking, intriguing woman."

I glanced over at him, having a hard time not returning his laugh. The good-looking comment was definitely gratuitous, but it was working. We continued our hike at a slow pace, side by side.

"How far are you on figuring out what *the more to life* is that you're looking for?" he asked.

"Not far at all. It's been a little hard to be contemplative in Cal's junkyard."

"Oh, I don't know. You could start your own New Age movement, rusted metal meditation."

"The guru of grime," I added, tucking a stray curl up under my cap. "One thing I do know, though, is whether I ultimately end up in New York or somewhere else, I want to build a life that's meaningful. I want to do work that matters, that takes me out of myself. L.A. is one of the most narcissistic places on the planet. It oozes conceit, and that has disturbed me for a very long time. So, no." I looked directly at him. "My story won't end like Dorothy's. I won't be going back home."

"Okay. Good to know." Noah nodded his head and stared up into the sky. "We better pick up the pace. I want to find a spot to eat before we head into the Narrows. You hungry?"

"Oh yeah, always." I took his okay as approval and an end to the conversation. Apparently, we were moving on to other territory, literally and figuratively.

Finding a fairly flat rock a few more minutes up the trail, Noah spread out the food he had brought along–turkey sandwiches with cranberry sauce and brie on sourdough bread, fruit salad, and oatmeal raisin cookies. Yummy. Why the guy was still single was a wonder.

"You ready to do this thing?" Noah asked, stuffing our trash into his backpack when we had finished.

"Sure." I stood up.

As we sloshed our way up the Virgin River and through the Narrows, it didn't take long to adapt to hiking in water. With cliff faces leaning in at perilous angles right above our heads, as if they were going to fall into each other at any moment, it was a magical place that seemed to defy the laws of physics. I loved it.

There was no conversation between us for quite several minutes. The place, as with all great cathedrals, both man-made and natural, called for quiet.

I don't know if it was the walking through water thing, but about twenty minutes into the Narrows I realized that my pee problem was beginning to kick in. My number one priority in choosing activities of any kind, but particularly travel, is proximity to immaculate indoor plumbing. Looking around me, I was pretty sure I wasn't going to come up with a loo in that locale. But, how was I going to explain that to Noah without embarrassing myself?

"Uh, excuse me, Noah," I ventured, as I watched him lead the way through a low point in the river. "I don't suppose there's a public restroom anywhere up ahead?"

Staring at me as my question registered, he answered, "Noooo."

"How about an In and Out Burger?" I smiled, hoping levity would cover my humiliation.

"Are you still hungry?"

"No. They have really clean bathrooms."

Noah smiled, then stepped away from the overhanging rock and stared up at the sky. "Clouds are starting to stack up. We should head back down anyway."

"Clouds?" I had been concentrating so hard on the river and rock formations I hadn't been paying any attention to what was above me. But, sure enough, there were clouds, as promised. "Do you think it's going to rain on us?"

"Probably." He crossed in front of me to lead us back the way we had come.

"Okay." I thought about the monsoon comment. "Hard?"

"Maybe."

"Do we need to pick up the pace?"

"We'll be okay. We're not far from the Riverside Walk. There's no danger. We might get a little wet is all. Let's throw on our jackets."

Wet was an understatement. What started out as a few drops quickly became a downpour. By the time we made it back down the Riverwalk Trail to the Temple of Sinawava, everything not covered by my rain jacket was soaked through.

The only benefit was if I had peed my pants, no one would have noticed.

After a run to the bathroom, I joined Noah in the line for the shuttle. "I'm a believer," I said, as we stepped on the bus, our jeans clinging to our legs.

"Oh, yeah? In what?" Noah pulled off his cap and ran his fingers through his hair as he scooted into a window seat.

"Monsoons. My first one." Hesitating before I sat down, I asked, "You sure they want us on this thing in our wet clothes?"

"It's just water. Happens all the time. And it's a long walk back."

"It's a long *ride* back to Harmony, too. I'd like to try to dry off a bit before we get into your truck."

"There's always the lodge."

"Do you think they have dryers there?" I scooted in next to him.

"No, rooms."

"Rooms?"

He turned to look at me, his eyes sparkling.

"Oh, rooms," I said, a little too old to be coy about what I was certain he was suggesting. "Hmm." Looking into and then past the hot ice blue of his eyes to the hair curling down behind his ears, I was mighty tempted. Oh boy, *what to do?* I dragged my eyes from his neck to the scenery out the window behind him.

"It's just a couple of stops away." He reached out his hand, turned mine over and rubbed my palm with his. Jeez, even his callouses were sexy.

Bending in, he pulled my baseball cap off my head, lifted the curls from my shoulder and kissed the hollow of my neck. "Okay, that's not fair," I whispered in his ear.

"All's fair," he whispered back then moved his lips higher up my neck.

That did it. I was toast. "I can think of worse ways to spend a rainy afternoon," I said into his ear.

"I can't think of a better way," he said softly into mine as he squeezed my hand.

CHAPTER FIFTEEN

The rain had let up and the light was fading by the time we climbed into Noah's truck for the ride home, thankfully. The lovemaking had been even more yummy than Noah's lunch. Back in the real world, bouncing along through Utah's vast empty spaces, I was happy to have the darkness to mask my discomfort at having given in to casual sex with the first guy who came along after Harry. And, with very little hesitation, I reminded myself.

Jeez. I had always prided myself on not being the casual sex type. Was I that desperate? Or, was it Noah? I took a quick glance at his profile. That whole cowboy persona of his certainly sucked me in. If I had been around in the sixties when the ads ran, I would have been dead from lung cancer for sure.

Noah seemed perfectly content to ride along in the quiet of the night, lost in his own world, and so I did the same. The last thing I wanted was a discussion about what had just happened, and the deeper meaning of it all.

As we neared Harmony, Noah reached over, ran his hand down my arm to my hand and tugged me over so I was pressed against him. Looking over at me, even in the dim light, I could see his eyes soften.

Stopping the truck after nosing into Cal's gate, Noah turned to face me. Combing the hair behind my ear with his fingers, he softly kissed me, first on my forehead, then on each eyelid and finally on my lips.

Wow. He was good.

"I'll walk you in," he said as he pulled back.

Opening my eyes, it took me a beat to come out of my cozy haze and realize what he had said. "Oh, no." I cleared my throat. "I'm good." Scooting across the bench seat, I reached for the door handle.

"I'll get that for you," he offered, starting to open his own door.

"No need." I hopped down from the truck then leaned back in. "Thank you ... for everything."

"Thank *you*."

Stretched out on his side by the door of the RV, Mr. Bumbles lifted his head as I approached. "Did they wear you out, boy?" I bent down and scratched him behind his ear. Standing up, he thumped his tail back and forth and put his front paws on the first step. It was past his dinnertime, and as food was the main highlight of his day, he couldn't get in the door fast enough.

I called V.A. while I was rummaging around putting Mr. B's meal together. Her phone went right to voicemail. Darn. I was anxious to find out how things went with Ruthie. Leaving her a message to get back to me right away, I decided to walk down to Dusty's. I wanted to find out if Dori was still there and whether or not she knew what had happened.

Alice was on the bed, right where I left her. Amazing. Rubbing my hand over her considerable fur-lined belly, I thought I was definitely going to have to put her on a diet and exercise regimen when we reached New York. It was either that or she was going to be in serious contention for the fattest cat in the land.

The aroma of grilled onions, coffee, and apple pie washed over me as I walked through the door of Dusty's. Not exactly a fusion of flavors that would make *Food and Wine* magazine's pages, but anyone who says their mouth doesn't water when they smell that combo is lying. I was suddenly very hungry.

Well, it *had been* a vigorous day.

The restaurant was still half full of the Saturday night crowd–three gray-haired couples at tables for two, and two groups in the larger booths. I slipped onto one of the stools at the counter, anticipating that it might be a while before I could talk to Dori because she was busy running between tables.

Poking his head under the divider between the kitchen and counter area and noticing me sitting there, Dusty smiled in recognition, and called, "You know what you want, Missy?"

"Absolutely," I smiled and called back. "Buffalo Bolognese, of course."

"Sure thing. Dori will get your drink order in two shakes."

"No hurry," I said as his face disappeared back into the kitchen.

The diners were down to just one couple by the time I finished my dinner. While clearing my plate, Dori agreed to tell Luke to head on home without her so we could talk. I moved over to a booth.

Sliding into the opposite seat, Dori pushed a mug of coffee over to me then took a sip of her own.

"Decaf?" I asked, nodding at the cup.

"Yes."

"Good. I don't want to be up all night." Reaching for the basket of coffee creamers at the end of the table, I asked, "Was Francis able to get a phone to Ruthie?"

"No." She loosened her hair from a purple ribbon she had used to tie it back. "V.A. told Francis that Samuel refused to bring Ruthie into her office. He was even nastier than usual, and hung up on her."

"Do you think he suspected something? Could someone have told him about our plan?" I poured the contents of the tiny half-and-half container into my cup.

"No. Not possible. The women in our group know how important it is to get a phone to Ruthie."

"Now what?" I exhaled.

"Now, we wait and hope we somehow hear something."

"How's that possible? Samuel seems to have his flock locked up tighter than King Midas' purse."

"I know. But, there are a few in the group who still have some contact with the women inside. We'll just have to see if we can get through to any of them to get word on Ruthie."

"Good luck on that one." I blew on my coffee and relaxed back into the booth.

Dori narrowed her eyes at me. "There's something different about you."

"What?"

"You have some color in your cheeks, and you seem more relaxed than normal."

Concentrating on not adding even more color to my cheeks, I forced my thoughts away from my day with Noah. "The color of my cheeks is freckle brown like they've always been. And, I'm almost always relaxed."

"Right. Guess again. I didn't have to be with you five minutes before I figured out we operate in the same mode, which is more like *almost never* relaxed. No, that's not it." She lifted her coffee to her lips. "I'd say it has more to do with your date with Noah."

"And, how do you know I was with Noah? Is there some Harmony twitter queen I don't know about who tweets what everyone in this town is doing at any given time?" Now, I did have color in my cheeks.

"Calm down. Don't ruin your buzz, woman. As you may have noticed, there aren't a lot of us around here. Keeping tabs on each other is what we do for entertainment."

"If that's your idea of fun, I'd sign up for cable or, better yet, find another town."

"Already have. As I told you, Luke and I are moving to L.A. very soon, I hope."

"That's right. Beaches."

"Beaches are part of it. I can't wait to tell this town, bye-bye. It's sucking my skin and soul dry. But, it's really more about getting an education that will prepare me for a job that doesn't involve the words, 'May I take your order, please.' Preferably work helping women. I figure in a place as big as L.A. there are bound to be more opportunities than in Southern Utah."

"No kidding. From what I've seen, you have more of a chance of advocating for women's rights in Syria than here."

Dori turned her legs to the side and kicked off her sandals, scooted to the end of the booth, leaned against the wall, and stretched her legs out. "They get sore." She reached down and rubbed her calves.

"I'll bet. Mind if I join you?" I asked, bending down to pull off my own sandals.

"Go for it."

"My bod's feeling that hike we took today." I copied Dori's position.

"Right, hiking." Dori turned up the corner of her mouth. "If Noah was ten years younger, I'd be the first in line to do a little hiking with him myself."

I started to protest, but looking over at Dori's don't-try-to-fool-me stare, I finally just gave in and laughed.

"Is he as hot as he looks?"

"Oh, yeah," I admitted.

"It's been so long since I've had a date."

"I'm surprised you could find one at all."

"Thanks."

"I don't mean it that way. I meant, who on God's earth would you find around here to date?"

"You pretty much need to get to St. George, but even there the choices suck. Baby boomers are moving there in droves. Think they've found paradise. And, I don't plan on dating any of them."

"Well, there are definitely plenty of men in L.A. your age. But, do you have any second thoughts about leaving the work you've started with the women here? At your meeting, they

FINDING HARMONY · 203

seemed pretty dedicated to helping the victims of scumbags like Samuel."

"They are, and that's what makes my going okay. They'll do just fine without me. I've been living in the same area, dealing with polygamy from the inside and outside my entire life, and I need to move on." Dori thumped the table for emphasis.

"I can certainly relate to the moving on thing." I studied the worry lines already forming between her young brows.

"Yeah? So, what's your story, anyway? What are you running from?" She picked up her mug and took a sip.

"I'm not running *from* anything. Like you, I spent my whole life in one place. I guess you could say I became uncomfortable with being comfortable. So, I gathered up what little courage I have and, for once in my life, did the hard thing. Make any sense?"

"Definitely. Sounds like divine discontentment. I read that somewhere and it stuck with me."

"I like that. I'm *divinely* discontent–a lot better than frustrated and fed up."

"So, what are your plans?" Dori set her mug back down and adjusted the folds of her skirt.

"Well ..." I scratched the back of my neck. "For starters, I'll probably be doing the same type of work in New York I did in L.A."

"Which is?"

"Editing."

"That doesn't sound very life-altering." She frowned.

"No. But, it's a way to support myself."

"Okay, so being an editor is what you think you *have* to do, but what is it you *want* to do?"

"What are you, my guidance counselor?"

"I told you, I plan on being an advocate for women. Consider this practice. You make this big move, say you want to do the hard thing, but here you are planning to do exactly what you were doing before, just in a different place."

"Well, I gotta eat."

"Yeah, but what are your big dreams?"

Settling back against the wall, I looked over at her penetrating black eyes. "Okay. You asked. Here it is. The only reason I ended up as an editor is because I didn't have any success at supporting myself as a writer. The frustration is that writing's something I've always loved and needed to do. I get really cranky if I am away from it too long. I also know I'm good at it. I know I can reach people and help people through my writing."

"But, who?"

"That's just it. I don't know yet. I keep thinking that someday it will hit me. I will hear something or see something, and have one of those aha moments you read about. Kind of like being zapped by a fairy godmother."

"I don't believe in fairy godmothers."

"Yeah, I bet you don't. So, were you born an old lady, or did it just come on as a result of that less-than-perfect childhood of yours?" I smiled.

"I'm pretty sure I was born this way." She relaxed her face and smiled back.

"That would have been my guess."

"I don't believe in waiting for aha moments either, by the way. While you're doing all that waiting, the real moments, the ones where you could be making something happen, pass right by."

"Wow." I slid my feet to the floor and faced her. "You're quite the thinker, Dori. Lucky will be the women who cross paths with you."

"Yeah, thanks." She looked uncharacteristically embarrassed at the compliment. "Now, I just have to figure out how to support us in L.A."

"I may be able to help you out with that."

"Really?"

"Yeah, that is if you think you want to keep working as a waitress while you're going to school."

"That's what I was planning on. If I could get a job at a popular place, I should be able to make pretty good money in tips. What do you have?" she asked.

"I can make a call to my ex, Harry. One of his best friends owns a restaurant on Hollywood Boulevard. It stays very busy. And, the best news is that it's near a subway stop."

"Is that a big deal?"

"Oh, yeah. If you have to commute by car, forget it. Your money wouldn't last two months with having to spend it all on the gas it takes to sit in bumper-to-bumper traffic." I covered my mouth to stifle a yawn. "I think the subway even has reduced prices or free passes for college students, but you'll have to check on that."

"I'll look it up online." Dori straightened up and reached down to put on her sandals, then slid to the end of the booth. "When can you make that call?"

I pulled my cellphone out of my purse and checked the time. "I'll call Harry on my walk back to the RV."

"Good. I'm off tomorrow. He can reach me anytime."

Dori was definitely not the shy retiring type.

I had avoided calling Harry all week, and hadn't even returned his last text. I didn't want to have the discussion with him as to why, a week later, I was still a stone's throw from L.A. Harry was a natural-born worrier, and he probably would have insisted on driving up to help me out. Our breakup had been rough, but fortunately we started talking again right before I left. When I envisioned my move, I had thought it would be a laser-clean break with L.A. But, how do you dam a memory stream of places and people deeply rooted in your heart? You don't. And, you shouldn't.

Harry picked up on the first ring, and after a round of twenty questions, I moved on to the purpose of my call. He was happy to help Dori out. I knew he would be. He was a giving guy.

Looking around at the dark street, I recalled that the last time I was in this situation, the Bailey boys had come along. I quickened my pace, happy that Cal's gate was only a few yards away.

Hearing the sound of an engine behind me, I moved even faster, thinking, Oh no! It can't be! I glanced over my shoulder, and when I saw it was Noah's truck, I sighed in relief. He pulled over and I walked around to the driver's side.

"My gosh. You scared me. What are you doing here?"

"You caught me." He pulled his hat off and set it on the seat beside him.

"Okay?"

"I stopped by V.A.'s for a spell, and as I was leaving, I noticed the Bailey boys driving by. Thought I'd better make sure they weren't headed your way to give you more trouble. Making a phone call?" He nodded at the phone, abruptly changing the subject before I had a chance to respond.

"Yeah, but all through." I slipped it into my purse, not wanting to go into an explanation of my conversation with my ex.

"I'm walking you in this time." He turned off the engine and started to open the door, not allowing a response from me.

Stepping out of his way, I didn't resist. With the Bailey boys out on the prowl and Cal away, I was fine with being tucked into the junkyard.

I lit our way through truck and car parts to the RV with the small LED flashlight from my key chain. "Charming little hideaway I've found for myself, don't you think?"

"A real beaut." He placed his hand on my back as we navigated around a large tire.

As we approached the motorhome's door, we found Mr. Bumbles engaged in one of his favorite activities, scratching behind his ear with his back foot, his collar and I.D. tags jingling.

"You going to be okay here tonight?" Noah asked as I turned to face him.

"Oh, sure. Mr. Bumbles may not seem like it, but he can be a ferocious guard dog when called upon."

"Right." Noah smiled, while Mr. B shifted his eyes from one to the other of us, looking a little embarrassed by the attention.

"Well, thanks again." I fished for my keys in my pocket to mask that sudden first date awkwardness I was feeling, even though we had gone far past the first date stage at the Zion Lodge. "You can find your way back to the truck?" I continued, head down, still fishing.

"I'll be fine." He tugged my hand out of my pocket and lifted my chin. Using both hands to comb the hair back off my face, he dipped his head, pressed his body into mine and kissed me, softly at first, then with a force that sizzled my nerve endings.

What had I gotten myself into? I wasn't quite sure, but a part of me was certainly going to be reluctant to get itself out–yeah, the part that had absolutely nothing to do with my intellect.

"Well, good-night, again," he whispered.

"Night," was all I could manage to whisper back.

CHAPTER SIXTEEN

Upon awakening, I was in an uncharacteristically perky mood for very early on a Sunday morning, so decided to take Mr. Bumbles for a quick walk before breakfast. While heading in the opposite direction from town, an area I hadn't explored other than my one time at Dori's, I was for the first time calculating the *hours* rather than the days I had remaining in Harmony. Forty-eight, I figured, with my newfound confidence in Cal. Maybe a little optimistic, but even if I couldn't leave until Tuesday afternoon, I still planned on putting a few dozen miles between myself and the nightmare of the last week.

Nightmare was a little unfair, considering my day in Zion. The park is as close as a person can get to heaven on earth. And Noah, well he was pretty heavenly himself. He was definitely going to be hard to leave behind, but looking over at the twisted chain link fence surrounding a stucco shack, I concluded he was about the only thing I would regret leaving.

A few minutes down the road, I noticed a small figure far off in the distance running toward me. Immediately sensing it was not someone out for a morning jog, I stepped up my pace.

As she came closer, I realized that it was Angela. Angela? What was she doing out there? Clearly intent on finding out for himself, Mr. Bumbles tugged on his leash and dragged me toward her.

When we approached her, I had to shout her name twice before she stopped running. Hurrying over, I squatted down so that we were at eye level. "What's the matter, honey?" I asked, putting my hand on her bony shoulder.

"Ruthie, it's Ruthie." She looked toward town. "They need to help her." She started to step around me, but stopped as Mr. Bumbles nudged her hand with his nose. Looking down at him then over at me, she repeated, "They have to help her."

"Why? What's going on, Angela?" I gently wrapped my hands around her upper arms so she would focus on me.

"She's sick. There's lotsa blood."

"Okay." I stood up, my heart pounding. "We'll go get help." Grabbing her hand in one of mine while holding Mr. B's leash in the other, I started off at a slow run, sorting through my options. I knew from town talk that Doctor Schrum would be of no help, so I decided my best bet was to get to Dori's, which was only a few minutes away.

Knocking hard on Dori's door, worried she might still be asleep, I waited, looking down at Angela's wispy blonde hair. So little. How did she summon the bravery to escape the meanies she lived with and run all that way?

Dori cracked the door open, dressed in flannel pajama bottoms and a t-shirt. The confused look on her face immediately became concern as she set her eyes on Angela. "What's happened?" she asked, ushering us in.

"Ruthie's sick. She's bleeding. You need to help her," Angela's voice cracked as her tiny body started to shake.

Looking at me over the top of Angela's head, Dori's eyes widened. Kneeling down, she pulled her into her arms. "It'll be all right, Angela, we'll get help, but we need to hurry. Where is she?"

"At home. Upstairs. In bed."

"Who's with her?"

"Mother Helen and the doctor, but he can't help."

"Okay, then. You wait here with Sydney. I'm going to get my clothes on."

Dori flew out of her room, still buttoning her top. "I called Emergency, but they'll be coming from St. George, so it's going to take a while. I'll borrow my neighbor's car, pick Francis up because I may need her help, then head over to the compound." Grabbing her purse, she reached for the door. "Call V.A. and tell her to get over there quick. She's the closest thing we have to a doc."

"No!" Angela cried out, lost in Dori's haste to be on her way. "Don't leave me! I want Ruthie!" She started to sob.

"It's okay." Dori turned back and hugged Angela to her legs. "You go on with Sydney and Mr. Bumbles right now, and ..."

"No! I want Ruthie!" Angela pulled out of Dori's grasp and started for the door.

"Okay, okay." Dori took her hand. "You can come with me, but when we get there, if we're going to help Ruthie, I need you to do what I say. Can you do that?"

Angela nodded her head.

"But, what about Luke?" I realized he must be in his room.

"He's fine. On the computer. Let's go."

V.A. arrived at Cal's within ten minutes of my phone call, having given me no choice but to go with her to Samuel's. She said she wanted reinforcement, as she was not expecting to be received with open arms.

No kidding. There was no saying "no" to V.A., but I was pretty sure I was about the last person that Samuel wanted to see. I was not going to be of much help with Ruthie, either, when even having my blood drawn makes me woozy.

When we pulled up in front of Samuel's house, Mother Helen was blocking the doorway, engaged in an animated conversation with Dori and Francis. Angela was standing behind Dori, using her as a shield.

V.A. was out of her truck and on the porch before I could get out of the cab. I hurried up behind her just in time to hear her say. "Show me to Ruthie, now," in a tone that brooked no argument.

When Mother Helen hesitated, V.A. pushed past her and through the door. Using her like an offensive lineman, we followed right behind.

I trailed V.A., Dori, Angela, and Francis up the stairs, with two sets of footsteps right on my heels. Creepy.

At the landing, V.A. turned back to Angela. "Where is Ruthie, sweetheart?"

Angela pointed to the end of a very long hallway. V.A. navigated it in a few long strides and disappeared through the door.

Following V.A. to the threshold, Dori, who had been holding Angela's hand, bent down. "We're going in there now, love, and see how Ruthie's doing. I want you to stay right here with Sydney."

"But ..." Angela started to protest.

"You told me you'd mind what I said, remember?"

Angela nodded her head.

"Okay, now." Dori put Angela's hand in mine. "Sydney will take good care of you. You just hold on tight to her."

Although she was speaking to Angela, Dori was clearly signaling to me that my assignment was to make sure none of the inhabitants of the household whisked Angela away from me. I was not looking forward to a wrestling match with Mother Helen, so was relieved when she and another woman with a matching braid followed Dori and Francis into the room.

They left the door open enough for me to see that Samuel was standing at the end of a bed, arms crossed, spitting fire up at V.A. However, he looked far less imposing than in my other encounters with him, as V.A.'s towering height and shoulder width emasculated his cartoonish build.

"You don't belong here!" he barked into V.A.'s face.

"No. *You* don't belong here, Samuel," she snapped back. "You belong in prison, and that's where you damn well will be going if something happens to Ruthie." She gestured to the bed. "Now, find yourself a corner and start praying to whatever god that warped brain of yours concocted. When the authorities show up they're going to be asking a whole lot of questions."

Samuel stood his ground for a few seconds, contemplating his next move. I thought for sure he'd hit her, but she must have gotten to him, because he dropped his arms and turned for the door.

Realizing he was heading right for Angela and me, I grabbed her around the shoulders and stepped behind the door, hoping he would pass us by.

No such luck.

He'd seen us.

Reaching out to grab Angela, he sneered, "Get your hands off her!"

"No!" I stepped in front of her and shoved his arm.

With lightening reflexes, he grabbed my wrist. Shrinking back from the wrath in his eyes, I realized it was actually me who was going to be hit. I raised my free hand for protection, when Samuel suddenly released his grip on my wrist, groaned, and buckled to his knees.

Confused, I looked over to find Dori standing over him. "God, I've been wanting to do that for a long time." She rubbed her foot. "I knew those self-defense videos would come in handy someday."

"Now, leave us alone," she said to the top of Samuel's head, then turned to us. "You better come inside." She stretched her arm out and gestured for us to step into the room. "Just keep Angela way back, okay," she whispered as I passed her.

"Sure." I nodded.

Fortunately, it was a very large dormitory-like room, with several beds lined up in a row. I walked Angela to the farthest one from Ruthie's bed and patted it for Angela to hop up.

Climbing up on the bed behind her, I blocked her view. Never ever without my purse strapped to my side, I pulled it over my head, set it on Angela's lap, and opened it, hoping to entertain her with the contents.

One by one, running through my makeup counter's worth of half-used lipsticks, I let her draw with them on a worn notebook, while keeping my ear trained on what was going on behind me.

At the sound of a male voice, I twisted my head around to see an old guy with white hair and red-rimmed eyes, who I hadn't noticed when I walked in, speaking to V.A. from a chair in the opposite corner of the room. She was shooting questions at him from where she stood at the side of the bed, and appeared none too happy with the response. Finally gesturing as if she wished to sweep him out of her sight, she turned back to Ruthie.

The man, who I assumed was the infamous Doctor Schrum, slouched in his chair and stared at the floor, his arms dangling between his knees, his mind off call. From the looks of the guy, he had more than earned his reputation as not having been *on call* for a very long time. Why Samuel would have even had him come, I had no idea.

My attention drawn to the bed, I couldn't see much, as Dori and Francis blocked my view. From Ruthie's groans and the concerned expression on V.A.'s face, however, things could not have been going very well.

Mother Helen, who had left the room, swept back in with her arms full of linens. I turned my attention back to Angela, praying for the paramedics to show up very soon.

In what seemed like an hour, but must have been more like fifteen minutes, there was a loud whirring and thumping overhead. I turned my head around to see Dori staring up at the sky through the window. "Finally. They're here."

"Helicopter," she added, responding to the inquisitive looks on the other faces in the room. "I told them they'd better send one. I just wasn't sure they would."

In the controlled chaos that followed it was impossible to keep Angela back from it. It was natural for her to be both repelled by, and attracted to the terrifying activity. I prayed that somehow someday the strength I sensed within her would pull her away from the grip of the psychopaths that were raising her.

As the paramedics transferred Ruthie to a stretcher, V.A. was right there. "I'll be riding along," she told them. They didn't question it.

"Drive my truck to the hospital," she called over to me. "Dori will tell you how to find the place." Reaching into her pocket, she tossed her keys.

"Sure." I grasped them in both hands, as V.A. followed the paramedics out of the room.

"We'll catch a ride with you after I drop my neighbor's car off." Dori motioned to Francis, who nodded her head at me. "Meet me at my place."

"Okay."

Looking down at Angela then over to Mother Helen, who was standing fixed to the floor next to a pile of bloody linens, Dori called her name, and said, "We're leaving now."

Apparently Mother Helen didn't think it warranted comment. She just stared at us.

"Angela," Dori reached for her hand. "Why don't you go along with…" She glanced over at the other woman from the household, who had been watching in morose silence the entire time we had been there, and asked, "What's your name?"

Looking over at Mother Helen before she answered, she said, "Agnes."

Walking Angela over to her, Dori said, "Why don't you go along with Agnes? I'll bet you haven't had any breakfast."

"On your way now," Dori prodded when Agnes didn't move.

Looking one last time at Mother Helen, Agnes finally left the room with Angela in tow.

"We're leaving Angela in your care." Dori walked over to Mother Helen. "But, that doesn't mean we trust you'll do right by her, or this is over."

"We don't need your trust," Mother Helen said, with flat eyes and a flatter voice, finally finding her tongue, "or, your help."

"Oh, really? Did you think Doc Schrum was going to help Ruthie?" She jutted her arm in the direction of his chair. I looked over, surprised he was still sitting there with the same incoherent demeanor.

"Do you think she stood a chance of surviving at all without our help? And Angela was the only one of you with brains enough to know that. We got here so late Ruthie still might not make it."

Dori moved within twelve inches of her. "There's absolutely no way you're going to be allowed to carry on, life as usual, when people find out what you did to that girl. No one in their right mind is going to trust you with the responsibility of other children." Dori turned away in disgust.

"We *will* see you at the hospital, right?" Francis spoke up.

Not answering, Mother Helen managed to retain her blank stare.

Dori and Francis frowned at her and left the room, passing Patrick as they went.

"Patrick," I said. "Who called you?"

"No one. I spotted the helicopter heading this direction and figured they weren't out for a joyride."

"You know then that Ruthie is on her way to the hospital in St. George?"

"Yes. One of the women downstairs told me."

"V.A. is with her."

"That's good; no one better in an emergency."

"Ruthie's condition appeared critical, at least from what I could tell."

"They have a top medical staff at the hospital. She'll be in good hands."

"I hope so," I said, nodding in Doctor Schrum's direction. "The medical help around here is worthless."

Patrick looked over then crossed to the corner to stand in front of the good doctor, who still hadn't changed from his slumped position.

When Patrick said his name, the doctor continued staring at the floor, as if he didn't hear, then mumbled something that sounded like, "Glory, glory, glory, I tried."

"What's he saying?" I asked Patrick.

"I'm not sure. I'm going to take him home."

"But, what about Samuel?"

"Yes?" He bent to grab the doctor's arm to encourage him to stand up.

"Aren't you at least going to question him?"

"If I can find him."

"He's not downstairs?"

"No, and when I inquired about him, the women had nothing to say."

"Jeez, he probably lit out of here to God knows where!" I felt my face flush in frustration at the thought of the cowardly little bastard getting away with murder if Ruthie died. "Can't you put out an all-points bulletin on him or something?"

"I called in an alert for law enforcement in the surrounding areas to be on the lookout for him. Maybe he'll show up at the hospital."

"*Right.*"

"Yeah. I wouldn't place a bet on it either."

"How about Mother Helen and the other women, then? They're almost as culpable. Shouldn't you at least question them?"

Pulling Doctor Schrum up and guiding him to the doorway, Patrick said, "I'm not worried about the whole lot disappearing, Sydney. I know how to do my job."

"Oh, sure. I know that." I followed him down the hall, embarrassed I had questioned his ability.

As we reached the entryway of the house, I caught a glimpse of several pairs of eyes staring at me from the end of the hallway that opened to the kitchen. Mother Helen was nowhere to be seen. I hoped it meant she was doing the right thing and on her way to the hospital. If not, I vowed I'd return and drag her there by her stinking braid.

CHAPTER SEVENTEEN

As Dori, Francis, and I walked into the waiting area of the hospital, there was no missing V.A. She was standing at the counter, looming over a young woman, who at the moment looked as if she might be reconsidering her career choice.

"What's happening?" Dori asked, as she stepped up to the counter beside V.A.

"Can't get a lot out of them." V.A. turned her eyes on the receptionist.

"Why not?"

"Not family." She stared at the woman, who quickly looked down at the papers in front of her.

"*I'm* family," Dori spoke up.

The woman lifted her head at that. "And how are you related?"

"Cousins."

"You are?" I asked from behind them.

"Yeah," Dori answered over her shoulder.

"You never said anything before."

"Not my favorite subject."

"So, what does that do for us?" V.A. asked the receptionist.

"Give me a minute." She stood up and disappeared through a set of doors behind her.

"How was Ruthie on the flight over?" Francis asked V.A.

"She was still losing a lot of blood, and going in and out of consciousness."

"Scary," I said.

"They were doing all they could, though, and were in constant communication with the hospital." V.A. tapped her fingers on the counter.

"They didn't let you stay with her, huh?" Dori said.

"No, the paramedics are a little looser with the rules than hospital personnel. I wasn't expecting them to let me into surgery. I'd just be in the way. But, it's clear as glass we're the only ones here right now for Ruthie, and there's no harm at all in letting us know what's going on." V.A. increased the volume of her voice when she noticed the receptionist returning to the desk.

"Okay," the receptionist said, still looking harassed, "I talked to the charge nurse, and she authorized me to inform you of Ruthie's condition."

"All right then, what is it?" V.A. said.

"She's still in surgery."

"That's it, Missy?" V.A. locked her eyes on her. Apparently, Missy was not a name that V.A. used exclusively for me, and apparently the receptionist was no fonder of it, because her response took on a definite edgy tone.

"I will let *you know* when *I know* more," she said then picked up the phone to make a call, turning her back to us.

A half an hour passed of fidgeting, pacing, and little conversation when through the glass doors entered Ma Odelia, gripping her walker, followed by Mama Miriam and Noah.

What were *they* doing there? It wasn't exactly a social gathering.

V.A. walked over and guided Ma Odelia to a chair across from us. Mama Miriam sat down beside her. As Noah took the chair next to mine, I cast a questioning glance his way. He took off his cowboy hat, set it on the chair next to his and nodded at me in hello, but didn't respond to the question on my face.

Miriam smiled softly at Francis, who was sitting on the other side of me. She then nodded at me and raised her hand at Dori, who was returning from the vending machine with a bottle of water in her hand.

"Anyone else want one," Dori offered, holding up the bottle.

"What's that you say?" Ma Odelia responded, way too loud for a hospital waiting room.

Oh no, not this again. I sighed. What was the matter with those people? It was just not the place or time.

Noah shifted in his seat, and when I looked over, set his hand on my arm, as if to stop me from speaking aloud what I was thinking.

Like I was going to! Looking down at his hand and back up at him, I pulled my arm back.

"She wants to know if you want a water," V.A. answered.

"Sure. I am a bit parched." She let go of her walker and reached up for Dori to hand her the bottle.

"You want one, Mrs. Loomis?" Dori said to Miriam.

"I'm fine, hon, thanks," she answered.

Dori walked back over to the vending machine to grab another water for herself.

"How is Ruthie?" Miriam touched the back of V.A.'s hand.

"She's still in surgery. That's all we know," V.A. said, looking over at the receptionist.

"Poor girl."

"Where's Ruthie's family?" Ma Odelia asked, handing the bottled water to V.A., and gesturing that she wanted her to remove the cap.

"That's a very good question."

"Samuel has disappeared," I said.

"Isn't he just like his daddy." Miriam frowned.

"You know the family?" I asked.

"Oh yeah, from way back. Our groups all arrived in the valley at about the same time."

"Were they all as miserable as Samuel?"

"Nah," Ma Odelia spoke up. "His granddaddy wasn't so bad."

"It was the change in Samuel's daddy that led to the split," Miriam added.

"Split?" I asked.

"Yeah, his daddy claimed a revelation," Miriam said. "He carved out a section of the women and children, built walls and fences, and the group's been hiding ever since."

"And, this is the result." Dori held her hand out in a sweeping gesture, compressing the sides of her water bottle.

Noticing a nurse pass through the doors behind the reception area, V.A. walked over to see if there was any word.

"She's out of surgery and in recovery." V.A. clasped her hands as she let us in on the news. "Thank the Lord."

"Amen," Miriam and Odelia said in unison.

"They said she's not out of the woods yet, but they're optimistic that she'll be fine," V.A. added.

"And the baby?" Dori asked.

"Stressed from the delivery and in the neonatal unit as a precaution, but also expected to be just fine."

"So, what is it?" I asked.

"Huh?" V.A. cocked her head at me.

"The sex of the baby?"

"Ha! I forgot to ask, by golly." She hurried back over to the counter. "A girl!" she called over to us.

A girl. Great. Another one destined for a life under the thumb of an ignorant evil man. God, I hoped not.

I got the impression Dori was on my same wavelength when she asked, "Do you think they'll let me see her now?"

"They said one family member can join her, and since the rest of her worthless kin haven't bothered to show up, I don't see why not," V.A. answered.

"Good," Dori picked up her purse and threw it over her shoulder. "Very good. If any of her group does show up, make sure the staff keeps them away as long as possible. As soon as she regains some strength, I want the chance to tell her there are other people who care more for her well-being than those she's living with right now. Samuel Vaullie is not her destiny. She has other choices she can make for herself and her little girl."

"Please let her know too, Dori, that Ma Odelia and I would like to take her back to our ranch to take care of her while she recovers." Miriam stood up to make her point.

"Do you think she'll go along with that?" I asked, knowing the grip Samuel had on her.

"What I think is that my judgment of human nature is usually pretty darn good," Miriam answered, "and I'll wager it's going to be a very long time before anyone lays eyes on Samuel again. We need to use this window to help as many of the women and children tied up with him as we can."

"Glad to have you on our side," Francis said, as Dori walked off to find her way to Ruthie. "The task at hand is not going to be an easy one, but I believe you're right about this opening. One like this doesn't come along very often, and we need to take advantage of it."

Okay, we were crossing into weird territory again. How was it that Miriam and Odelia, two polygamist women, were going to *save* Ruthie from polygamy? I had to grip the arm of my chair to keep from asking the question aloud. Looking over at Noah, he lifted his eyes, which had been focused on my white knuckles. I rolled mine at him, and he shrugged slightly, as if to say, it is what it is. But, what it *was* was nuts.

"I'm going to step outside and make a few phone calls so our group can start strategizing right away." Francis pulled her cellphone from her purse and stood up.

"Are you going to need a ride home?" V.A. asked.

"No, I'm sure I can get one from one of the women." She hurried out the door to the vestibule.

"How about you two? There's not a lot you can do right now. Do you want me to run you home?" V.A. said to Miriam and Odelia.

"Sure," Miriam said. "But, I'd like to come back when Ruthie can have visitors to make clear we truly want her and the baby to stay with us."

"We'll check back later this afternoon to find out when we can visit," V.A. said, then turned to Noah. "I do appreciate your bringing them all the way over here, Noah. They were very concerned."

"My pleasure." He reached for his hat.

Movement through the glass doors drew our attention to Francis, who was still standing at the entrance. She dropped her cellphone from her ear and called out to Mother Helen and Agnes as they marched by her. They didn't slow down.

V.A. moved swiftly to the doors in order to intercept the women as they entered the waiting room. Crossing her arms, she dared them to march past her. "So, you finally decided to show up." V.A. looked down on them.

"Are you going to let us by?" Mother Helen glared up at her, ignoring V.A.'s comment.

"No," V.A. said in a clipped tone.

That made them pause for a moment. Mother Helen dropped her guard long enough for us to notice she was a whole lot less sure of herself than she tried to put forth. She looked around the room as if searching for someone to help extricate V.A. from her path. "You have no right to stop us."

"Maybe not, but I'm going to anyway." Turning to the chairs that Noah and the rest of us had been preparing to vacate, she said, "I'd like you two to sit down for a minute so we can talk with you."

"Again, you have no right to stop us, and we have no intention of doing what you say." Mother Helen straightened her spine.

"I wouldn't be so ready to reject our request, Helen." V.A. softened her tone. "It may be the best offer you get. I'm not sure the police will bother to chat, once they get the full story of the risk you all took with Ruthie's life."

At the mention of Ruthie's name, Mother Helen's posture drooped slightly. "Do you know how she's doing?" she asked with genuine concern on her face.

"She and the baby both pulled through," V.A. answered.

Agnes, who was standing partially behind Mother Helen, sucked in her breath, and put her fist to her mouth to stifle a sob.

Mother Helen extended her hand back to grasp Agnes's arm, and set her jaw to keep her own face from crumbling.

"Now, come on over and sit down." V.A. took Agnes's elbow and led the two of them to the chairs. Noah and I moved away from ours. Between Francis, who had walked back in behind Helen, and the women in V.A.'s group, things were getting a bit crowded.

"Shall we be on our way?" Noah asked me, holding his hat to his side.

"I'd like to grab a soda first." I nodded to the vending machine. I had come that far with the melodrama, there was no way I was going to miss out on the next scene.

Noah frowned, but followed me across the room. As I slowly perused the soda selection, with one ear to the conversation going on behind us, he said, "I'd be happy to take you out for a bite to eat."

"Uh ha," I said, barely hearing him.

"It's way past lunchtime."

Standing up, I put my finger to my lips and nodded to the women.

His frown deepened.

Frowning back, I whispered, "I was dragged into this mess over the past week, and I want to hear what's said. You can go on, if you like."

"No, I'm not going to do that. In case you haven't done the math, I'm your ride, that is unless you'd like to bounce all the way back to Harmony in the bed of V.A.'s pickup."

"Oh, that's right." I put a dollar bill into the machine. "Just give me a few minutes."

"I'll be in my truck." He set his hat on his head, and strode out the door.

Miriam was speaking to Mother Helen and Agnes when I turned my attention back to their conversation. "We've known you since you were sweet little things, and somewhere in those hearts of yours you must understand that what has been going on in your household has put innocent young ones in the hands of evil."

"Look, we know it's going to take a lot of undoing to begin to make you see that the man you've been following all these years is concerned solely with his own demented needs," V.A. joined in, "but, so far as Ruthie and her baby are concerned, if they're to stand a chance, the ties to Samuel and your household have to be cut now, today."

"No." It was Agnes who spoke for them. "No. We love her. She's a part of the family." Her voice cracked.

"And if you love her, you'll walk out of here and let her have a chance at the life she deserves." V.A. looked from Agnes to Mother Helen.

"But, she'll think we abandoned her." Agnes's eyes began to tear up.

"Yes. At first, she will. But, there are people here," Miriam chimed in, nodding at Francis, "who will be there for her. And, eventually she'll come to realize what a good life is supposed to be like."

"We've had a good life." Mother Helen lifted her chin and stared defiantly from woman to woman.

"No Helen, you've just been brainwashed into thinking that." V.A. reached out and patted her arm.

She shrunk back a bit, but didn't pull her arm away.

"Listen." V.A. held Mother Helen's eyes. "You can fight us on this, but you're going to lose. Samuel has been living outside of the law and getting away with it almost his entire life, but not this time."

"Where is Samuel?" Ma Odelia asked, apparently having followed the conversation pretty well.

Mother Helen and Agnes exchanged a quick glance, but didn't respond.

"So, he's gone. And left you to deal with the fallout. If that alone doesn't convince you of the nature of his soul, I don't know what will."

"You need to go now." V.A. lifted her hand from Mother Helen's arm. "Go back to your house and take a stab at honesty. Talk with your group members. Look into the eyes of your children, and decide how you want the rest of your lives to play out."

"And, if at some point you'd like some help of any kind, call us." Francis held out a piece of paper with phone numbers on it to Mother Helen.

After staring at it for a few seconds, she took it and placed it in the pocket of her skirt.

At that point, I had seen enough to convince me there was a chance that life for Ruthie, her baby, and Angela would have a happy ending. A slight chance, maybe, but it was something. I quietly moved along the wall to the door.

CHAPTER EIGHTEEN

Sitting on Noah's porch, I gazed at the mesa off in the distance, admitting once again to myself that the vistas around Harmony were spectacular in scope and color. The strata of the cliffs were like a chocolate, strawberry, and banana trifle topped with a cloud of whipping cream. Wait. Or was that just my growling stomach conjuring up dessert before the main course as usual?

When we left the hospital, Noah suggested we have an early dinner at his place, rather than at a restaurant in St. George. I didn't object, as it was likely to be the last time I would lay eyes on him, and the lure of his Marlboro Man appeal had not waned at all. I didn't expect to find any ruggedly handsome cowboys in New York. Darn.

Pushing the screen door open with his hip, he carried two chilled glasses to the table. Trudy trotted out after him, circled the deck twice, then curled up at the top of the steps and tucked her snout under her paws.

"You sure I can't help you?" I asked.

"No. The meat for the tacos will be done in a few. Let's just enjoy our beers for a spell."

"Sure. Thanks." I lifted my glass and held it out to him. "Cheers."

Clinking his glass to mine, he echoed my toast, his eyes crinkling at the corners. Yes, I was definitely going to miss that face.

I took a long gulp, thinking as I always did when having a beer on a warm day, that there was nothing better to relax the attitude. Maybe it made me unrefined, but in a setting like this, I'd place the first swallow of beer over the first sip of wine any day.

"It looks like the women of Harmony are going to rally around Ruthie, maybe even be able to help Angela and some of the others." I set my glass down.

"They're determined."

"And, they have the advantage of having Samuel out of their way. Do you think he will ever show up?"

"Don't know." He set his glass down and leaned back in his chair. "Kinda doubtful."

"Yeah, I think so too." I picked up my glass and took a few more swallows. Returning it to the table, I was surprised to see the beer more than half gone. I was also surprised to discover I was feeling a bit woozy. But, with soda the only thing I had put in my stomach the entire day, it was no wonder.

"When do you expect to be heading out of here?" Noah asked.

"Cal told me before he left that he's going to start working on the motorhome first thing in the morning, so even by *his* clock you'd think it would be fixed by Tuesday midday."

"You'd think." Noah smiled.

"With my newfound confidence in Cal, I'm optimistic I'll be lumbering down the highway very soon. Let's just say that."

"Not going to stick around to see how everything plays out, as involved as you were over these past few days?" Noah stretched out his legs and crossed his ankles.

"It wasn't like I went looking for all your town's troubles." I scooted my chair around, leaned back and stretched my legs out next to his.

"No, but, you didn't shy away from them either."

"What else was I supposed to do with a week in Harmony?" I looked over at Noah then turned around, grabbed my glass off the table and took several swallows of my beer.

"I can think of something." He reached his hand out and rubbed it along the top of my thigh.

Shoot, he was tempting. I looked down at this hand then up into his eyes, which were focused on mine. While contemplating the wisdom of a last spin with him, his face suddenly blurred and the porch tilted. Sliding my legs back under me, I said, "I think I need to eat," and started to stand. Reaching out to place my glass on the table, I lurched into it instead. Noah caught my arm and righted me.

"I better sit down." I couldn't count on remaining upright.

Guiding me to the banquette in the kitchen, Noah held onto my arm until I was safely seated. Walking over to a cupboard, he grabbed a bag, dumped some trail mix into a bowl and set it on the table. "Get some of this in you." He pushed it in front of me. As I grabbed a fistful, he placed both of his hands on the table and leaned in, his face close to mine. "I do believe you are the first person I ever witnessed get drunk on one glass of beer."

"Blood sugar issues," I said between crunches, shrugging my shoulders. "Not my fault. No chance to eat."

"Or, just an act to put off going to bed with me." His eyes twinkled, then he kissed my forehead, stood up and walked over to the stove.

Good thing his back was turned because I was sure I was bright red.

Okay, so I did end up going to bed with him. All it took was four tacos, a salad, and a chocolate sundae, and my hunger drive mercifully stepped aside to let another demanding drive have its turn.

Lying in his bed, pressed to Noah's side, I absorbed the consummate contentment of skin on skin. How had one week in a brown little town in Southern Utah paint so colorful a canvas of people, images and events? Try as I might I knew they'd never become that fading reflection in my rearview mirror I had hoped for my entire time here.

How did I become attached to the sight and the scent and the feel of this man, with so little conscious thought and in so little time? How was I going to leave him? I sighed.

"Yes?" he asked, responding to my sigh.

"Okay, I admit it, I am." I ran my hand over his chest and down his arm.

"You am what?"

"*I am* curious about how all the stories here are going to end. It's like I've been caught up in a soap opera, and I'm walking out before the final episode airs. I never liked soap operas." I sighed again.

"So, stick around." He rolled away from me, propped a pillow behind him and leaned against the headboard.

Keeping myself covered with the sheet, I sat up, shifted to face him, bent my knees, and wrapped my arms around them. "Just like that?"

"Why not?"

"Oh, I don't know, maybe because I was supposed to be in New York days ago; and up until days ago I had never even heard of this place."

Smiling, he interrupted, "Most people haven't. And we like it that way."

"There's no work for me here, nothing for me to do, and I have no family or friends here."

"Cal would be very hurt to hear that." Noah's eyes twinkled. "And so am I."

"You're not friends, Noah, you're acquaintances."

He shifted his eyes to my breasts, which had become exposed when the sheet slipped down. "Acquaintances, huh?"

Quickly pulling the sheet up, I said, "Okay, I admit that some of you are more intimate acquaintances than others."

"Some?" Noah's smile broadened. "You've been busier than I thought."

"Well no, not *some*, I mean ..." I stumbled for words, putting my forehead to my knees. "You know what I'm trying to say." I raised my chin to look at him. "The point is, how can I possibly build a life here?"

"What is there for you to build a life around in New York? It seems to me that if your intention was to start over in a new place, that new place could be pretty much anywhere you choose."

"But, there's no work here, Noah."

"What kind of work were you going to be looking for in New York, again?"

"Editing. I have a good resume and some leads I plan to follow up on."

"So, that's your dream, to edit other people's work in New York."

"Of course it's not my dream. It's how I plan to support myself."

"So, what *is* your dream?"

"Jeez, you sound just like Dori. Harmony doesn't exactly strike me as a New Agey kind of place, yet you're the second person to want me to get in touch with my dreams."

"Do I look like a guru to you?"

"No." I studied the cut of his biceps, the sunbrowned tone of his hands and face, and the curl of his hair at his neck. If he did form a cult, however, God help me, I'd be first in line for the Kool-Aid.

"Look, all I'm saying is you're kidding yourself if you think shifting location is going to shift what's in here." He touched his finger to my chest.

"Yeah, yeah, Psych 101. I get it, but I disagree, in part anyway. You don't set out on a misadventure like this without a shift in here." I also pointed to my chest. "L.A. wasn't enough for me anymore. *My life* wasn't enough for me. There's something I need to do. The frustrating part is I can't begin to satisfy that need, because I don't have a clue what that something is. Right now, it's just a sense of uneasiness that will not be ignored. Erg." I groaned, grabbed the edge of the sheet, plopped down on my back, and covered my face with my hands. "I don't know, I don't know, I don't know. I guess I'm a mess," I mumbled through my hands.

Leaning over me, Noah pulled my hands away from my face. "Yeah, but you're an interesting mess."

"Interesting. Great. That's one of those weenie words that people use when they're too polite to say what they really think."

"Weenie words. See, now that's interesting." Noah smiled and bent in to kiss me, a long soft kiss. Wow. He had great command of my goose bumps.

When he finally pulled back, I said, "And then, on the other hand, there's a part of me that could just cozy up in this weird little town of yours and wile away the rest of my life eating buffalo Bolognese and pulling calves. Second thought, probably not the pulling calves thing." I smiled.

"No, if you care about your tailbone, you might want to leave the calf pulling to the experts. If you decide to stay, I'm sure Dusty will be happy to supply all the buffalo Bolognese you'd like. And, I'd be more than happy to come up with other alternatives to occupy your time."

"That's neighborly of you."

"We're a friendly lot around these parts." He grinned.

"I noticed."

CHAPTER NINETEEN

Driving down Main Street past Dusty's, the resolve I felt in the weeks before in designing a new life for myself was crumbling fast. With the thought of Noah's touch, a lingering comfort, the tug of security pulled hard on me. But, I had always chosen the safe route. That's why I set out on this journey in the first place–to for once in my life take the road less traveled. And, boy did I ever find one. I studied the silhouettes of the sparsely scattered buildings.

A few hundred yards shy of Cal's yard, two sheriffs' vehicles raced up behind Noah's truck, passed us at a high rate of speed and took a sharp turn down a road to the left.

"What was that?" I asked, shaken by the disturbance in the dead quiet night.

"I don't know, but we're going to find out." Noah took the same left, but at a much safer speed.

"What's down here?" I peered into the darkness through the passenger window.

"Just a house or two spread out over a lot of acreage." Noah concentrated on the taillights in front of us.

Turning right after about a mile, we followed the lights down a long gravel drive. "Do you know who lives here?" I asked as Noah pulled the truck over and turned off the ignition a few feet behind the other vehicles, which had parked in front of a low-slung ranch style house.

"I think it's Doc Schrum's place, but I can't be sure. My mom stopped taking us to him when we were really young. I haven't been down this road in years."

Ablaze with interior and exterior lights, the house illuminated the yard around it, a shabby collection of weeds, sage, and a few sorry cottonwoods. Adding to the intensity of the house lights, were the high beams from two additional cars, parked nose in to a partially fenced side yard.

As Noah and I stepped out of his truck and walked toward the side yard, we recognized the cars as those belonging to Patrick and the rookie deputy. From the splintered wood and planks haphazardly strewn on the ground, it was clear the fence had been torn apart in order to make room for their vehicles.

Walking past Patrick's car, I halted when I saw movement in the back seat. "That's Doc Schrum in there." I reached out to grab Noah's arm.

Noah slowed up, bending slightly so he could see into the car. "Yes, I believe that's him."

The doctor was sitting in pretty much the same pose as the last time I saw him in Samuel's house, shoulders slumped, eyes down. His arms appeared to be behind his back. "Is he in handcuffs?" I asked Noah in a whisper.

"Yeah."

"My God, what happened?"

"Let's take a look." Noah motioned for me to follow him between the car and the broken fence.

Standing halfway across the yard, engaged in conversation with the deputies we had followed to the house, Patrick looked up when he saw our movement and raised his hand to signal for us to wait.

Stopping, we noticed that a few feet beyond Patrick the rookie seemed to be digging a large hole. There were several piles of fresh dirt in the yard, indicating that at least one other hole had been dug.

Trembling, I moved closer to Noah. He put his arm around my shoulder and pulled me to his side.

After several minutes of waiting in silence, watching the surreal scene, the other deputies headed back toward their cars, and Patrick walked over to us. "Noah, Sydney." He acknowledged us with a slight nod of his head.

"Patrick," Noah said. "What's happened?"

"Gloria and Joannie." Patrick turned his head to look at the scene.

"The girls who disappeared?" I asked, my voice unnaturally high.

"Yes." He turned back to us.

"What about them?"

"We found them," he said, his brown eyes weary.

"There?" I pointed at the holes.

"Yes, I'm afraid so."

"No. How?" I moved away from Noah and took a step to cross the yard.

He pulled me back. "Hang on, Syd."

"But, I don't understand." A lump formed in the back of my throat.

"Let Patrick explain." Noah enclosed his hand around mine.

"When I was driving the doc back here this afternoon, he kept repeating, Glory, Glory, Glory, like at Samuel's. It took me awhile, but I finally figured out he was referring to *Gloria*." Patrick pushed his glasses up on the bridge of his nose. "I should have figured it out sooner."

Continuing, he said, "So, I settled him in his house, got some food in him, and started probing him as to why he was talking about Gloria. I guess the old man had carried the burden for so long he'd had enough."

"What did he tell you?" I asked, not sure I wanted to know the answer.

"He told me that Gloria and Joannie and their babies had died in childbirth, under his care. He tried to defend himself by saying he told Samuel they needed to take the girls to the hospital. He said Samuel threatened to kill him if he ever told anyone what happened, which may have been true. I wouldn't put it past Samuel."

"So, the girls and their babies are buried here?" Noah asked.

"Uh huh. We found one grave, and are working at finding the next one."

"How'd you know where to search?" Noah looked over at the rookie.

"Like I said, the doc was more than ready to relieve himself of the secret he's been keeping all these years. He told us that Samuel's nephews had buried them in the dark of the night. Clear out here, they probably figured no one would ever find them." Patrick took a deep breath. "And, they probably counted on Doc Schrum being so cowardly and rummy he'd never say a thing."

"So, Samuel *is* a murderer." I shivered.

"I'm afraid so."

"A murderer who is nowhere to be found."

"Oh, we'll find him. We haven't come this far just to have him get away with it. The other deputies are heading over to Samuel's compound right now to round up the nephews and make sure none of the other members of the household plan on taking any trips."

"It may take more than two men for that assignment," Noah turned in the direction of the drive as he heard the deputies' cars turn around on the gravel.

"They're calling for backup to meet them there," Patrick said.

"I can't believe Mother Helen and those other women stood by and let all this happen." My limbs began to shake, though it wasn't cold. "It's disgusting! No different than if they'd murdered those girls themselves! And they seemed so concerned about Ruthie. It was naive of me to think those women cared about each other." My eyes began to well up.

"In their own way, they probably do," Noah said softly, putting his arm around my shoulder and looking into my eyes. "But, they've been isolated from everything except Samuel's way for so long their thinking is warped."

"They're warped all right, but they're still responsible." I uncrossed my arms and turned to Patrick. "And, they should be held accountable for their crimes, just like Samuel. Will they be?"

"I'm sure some of them will, but it's going to take a long while to sort it all out."

"And, in the meantime, Samuel is probably headed for Mexico."

"That's a real possibility, but like I said, we'll do everything we can to see he's caught."

Sighing deeply, I turned to watch the rookie, who had just poured another shovel load of dirt onto a growing pile. "So, you solved your cold case?"

"Yeah, I suppose I did. Tough to feel any satisfaction when this is the outcome." He nodded at the open grave.

"But, the outcome is also that Samuel loses," Noah spoke up, his voice strong with conviction. "His desire was to toss those girls away as if they had never lived. You brought the memory of them back, and because of that I don't think the folks around here will be as inclined to tolerate the likes of Samuel ever again."

Hearing the kindness in Noah's voice, I thought, this is a good man.

"I appreciate your saying that, Noah." Patrick straightened to his full height and glanced over his shoulder at the crime scene. "I need get back at it."

Extending my hand, I said to Patrick. "It was a pleasure to meet you. And thanks for your help with the Bailey gang."

"Same here. Glad we could recover your Sandy Koufax, despite his being a Dodger." He enclosed his long fingers around mine.

"I'll be forever grateful for that. And, I *will* be following up on the Bailey boys' criminal career."

"Then, I may be hearing quite a bit from you, because there's a very good chance it's going to be a long and ugly one. Bye now, Sydney." He set his jaw, turned, and strode over to the graves.

Despite my claim to stay in contact with Patrick, as I watched him walk away, I wondered if when the Harmony page of my life turned I ever really would.

Picking our way through Cal's rust yard, Noah held tight to my hand.

Still shaky from the discovery at Doc Schrum's and overwhelmed by the foul trail of damage that Samuel left in his wake, I felt that old familiar knot of homesickness.

Homesickness. But, for what home? L.A.? Here? No. How could I be homesick when my idea of home was nothing but an elusive image?

Hard as I tried to force them back, by the time we reached my steps, tears had started to pour over my lower lids, and I was in serious danger of breaking out in sobs. Damn.

Sensing my anguish, Noah hugged me to his chest and stroked my back. Double damn. That did it. When I was like this, all it took was someone to be nice to me and I was a goner.

When my tears finally ceased flowing, and I had thoroughly dampened the front of Noah's shirt, I pulled back. "Sorry to fall apart on you." I wiped my face with the back of my hands.

"A natural reaction. This was no ordinary day."

"That's an understatement. Truly there have been times over the past week I've felt like I landed on another planet."

"There are actually a lot of us around here who are earthbound." Noah combed his fingers through the front of his hair. "You just happened across more than your fair share of those who probably should be sent to another planet."

"I'm not too sure about that. Even the non felons, Cal, V.A., Odelia, Miriam, are definitely not like anyone I've ever met before."

"But, that's part of Harmony's appeal."

"*Right.*"

"You think spending your time among dark-suited New York clones glued to their smartphones could possibly be more exciting than this?" He gestured to Cal's yard. I could just make out the twinkle in his eyes with the aid of the weak spotlights that Cal left on–his idea of security.

"You have a point there."

"So, how about it?" He put his hands around the small of my back and pulled me into him. "Why don't you stick around and give Harmony a chance. It might grow on you."

Feeling the warmth and strength of his torso, I knew it already had. I leaned back, better to see his eyes, and briefly succumbed to the idea of creating a life with this man on a foundation of iron laced, high desert soil. V.A., Cal, Patrick, Noah, these were good people living a simple life. What was so bad about that?

But no, I sighed. I just couldn't. Not now. Not yet. It was far too soon to abandon the goals I'd set for myself, to ignore the itch to explore the possibilities, whatever they may be.

"I can't." I relaxed my shoulders and let my arms drop from around his waist. "I just can't." I knew there was a very good chance I would regret abandoning *this* possibility.

Studying my eyes, he thankfully said no more. Bending his head, he kissed me softly. I responded, also softly at first. Then I slid my arms around his waist once again, and gave myself over to the moment, to the pleasure, and to the purity of being desired by this man.

CHAPTER TWENTY

Leaving Alice stretched out on the dinette, I followed Mr. Bumbles out the door. He was on a mission to meet up with his coonhound buddies for their morning sniffathon. I was on a mission to find Cal. He hadn't come near the motorhome, and it was already approaching nine o'clock. If he was going to fix the thing by tomorrow, he needed to get on it.

Taking a deep breath, well, not too deep–it was a junkyard after all–I calmed the already rising doubt about him keeping his word. My changed attitude about his competence certainly hadn't lasted very long.

Hearing noise coming from the garage, I entered through the left bay and spotted Cal bent over the workbench. Leashed to the bumper of a huge old sedan was an audience of the coonhounds. Their eyes riveted on Cal, they were as still as I had ever seen them, except for the quivering that rippled their fur.

Mr. Bumbles was there too, having found his pals, but clearly confused about the lack of enthusiasm at his arrival. After sniffing two of them with no response, he gave up, sat down, and looked back at me as if to say, "What's with them?"

Crossing over to Cal, I hesitated before I reached him, noticing the project he was working on wasn't made of metal.

"Cal?" I called softly, not wanting to be accused of sneaking up on him.

"Mornin'." He turned around to face me, his bloody hands gripped around a piece of whatever it was he slaughtered the day before.

"Morning." My eyes fixed on a very large slab of meat on the bench behind him.

"Pronghorn." He raised the glistening red chunk in his hand.

"Oh?" I didn't know whether to gag or say congratulations.

"Some hunters ain't fond of it. Say it's got too much of a sage taste. It's just cuz they don't know how to dress it out. You gotta skin it and gut it right away; get the cavity filled with ice, and keep it on ice 'til you're ready to butcher."

"Good to know." It was taking all I had not to turn and flee, especially with him flinging the meat in his hand around to punctuate his discourse. But, I needed the guy, and it would have been hypocritical of me to condemn Cal's hunting. I was an unapologetic meat eater.

"This guy was a real specimen," he continued, stepping over to a huge cooler. "Got him when he was nice and calm, grazing away peaceful like, another thing that makes the meat a lot sweeter. You take 'em down on the run, and the meat's not nearly as good."

As he bent down and pulled back the lid, I gasped and shrunk back. The entire head of the antelope was staring up at me through a mask of ice cubes.

Turning to look at me, Cal narrowed his eyes. "Somethin' wrong?"

"Uh, no." I cleared my throat, determined to keep him on my side. "It just, I didn't think, you know, you'd want the head."

"I'm not gonna eat it. Got a friend; does taxidermy. I'm savin' it for him."

"Thoughtful." I averted my eyes from the large glassy ones looking back at me from the cooler.

Closing the lid and straightening up, he said, "Just got a bit more butchering to do, then I'll get at your motorhome."

"Great." I tried not to look impatient. "Any idea how long it will take?"

"Well." He sucked in his breath through his bottom teeth. "Repair work's tough to predict, but I'm not anticipating any trouble, so should have her done tomorrow mornin' sometime."

"That would be wonderful," I said, thinking, *Glory Hallelujah!* "I'd like to be on the road midday, if possible. Put some miles between me and Harmony."

"Beats me why you're so anxious to leave," he said, once again giving me a scrutinizing stare. "You'd be hard-pressed to find country prettier than this." He pointed his chin at his yard.

Following his glance out the door, I thought he had to be talking about the landscape *outside* his rusted metal sculpture garden. "You do have some amazing vistas," I agreed, "especially around Zion, but I have to be on my way to New York. I'm way behind schedule."

"And there's another thing for ya about this place. Folks around here ain't in such a dang hurry like city folks, which goes a whole lot easier on the spirit."

"I noticed," I said, with more of an edge than I should have. Covering, I looked over at the coonhounds. "Your dogs are sure being good."

"They know the drill. No jumpin' and no barkin', or no treat."

"You've trained them well."

"Not hard when you got dogs as smart as these."

Noting Cal's proud look at them, I nodded in agreement, but was thinking I'd take Mr. Bumbles and his hang loose nature over those yelping bundles of hyperactivity any day. Turning to leave the garage, I said, "I'm going to take a long walk and then head into town to stay out of your way. Mind if I leave Mr. B here?"

"He's always welcome."

"Thanks. You have my cellphone number if you need me."

Sweaty from my walk, I called V.A. to ask about using her shower. She didn't have a lot of patients scheduled for the day, so she said it was okay to come on over.

Pulling on her screen door, which was still in serious need of a good oiling, I didn't bother to knock, knowing the screeching would bring her around.

"No Mr. Bumbles?" she asked, when she saw I was by myself.

"No. I left him behind to spend a last day with Cal's dogs. He's been having a great time with them."

"You oughta think about getting a pal for him. I'm sure Cal would be happy to help you out."

"Oh yeah, right, Bumbles, Alice, and a coonhound. Wouldn't that make for a great mix in the motorhome." I followed V.A. inside. "I bet we wouldn't get two miles down the road before Alice tried to claw her way out the window by way of my lap."

"Ha!" V.A. laughed. "I'd like to see that one."

Stepping out of the bathroom, I followed the sounds I heard coming from the kitchen. When I walked into the sunlit room, V.A. was taking a pitcher out of the refrigerator.

"Iced tea?" She set the container on the small oval dining table.

"Sure."

"So, you're leaving tomorrow." V.A. grabbed two glasses out of an upper cabinet.

Sitting down, I said, "Looks like it. Cal said he'd have the motorhome finished tomorrow morning, and this time I think he means it."

"Stranger things have happened." V.A. sat down across from me.

Pouring the tea into the glasses, she pushed one over to me. "Thanks." I held it up. "For everything this week, my tooth, the shower. I'd be one stinky mess without your help." I laughed.

"Couldn't have that." V.A. held up her glass and took a long sip. "You did have a busy week, Missy."

"The last thing I expected. Here I thought I was going to have a quiet few days making my way across country, with no one to talk to but my animals, then I hit Harmony. Who knew that this sleepy little town was anything *but* sleepy?"

"Harmony's not so different from any other place, I expect. Where there are people, there are always going to be the meek and the mighty, the kind and the cruel, the doers and the sitters. From the way you dove in up to your neck around here, Missy, I'd say you fall into the doer camp."

Thinking about her words, I couldn't keep up the pretense that my involvement over the past week was entirely forced on me. It was my choice to engage with Noah, Ruthie, Dori, and the rest, and I had decided it wasn't a bad thing. "I will take that as a compliment. It's just too bad the doing wasn't enough. The cruel got away with murder. You know they found Gloria and Joannie."

"Yeah."

"I thought you would." I rubbed the dew on the side of my glass.

"Samuel may not be in custody, but with the law after him, Ruthie being saved, and the opening Dori's group now has with the women and children in his cult, those are big things."

"You're right. Those *are* big things. I admire the focus and determination of that group."

"Not tempted to stick around and join them?"

"No. It's their crusade. I need to find my own."

"Just be sure when you decide to take up a fight it's for the right reasons. The world has more than its fair share of do-gooders running around thinking more about their ticket to heaven than the folks they should be serving." V.A. picked up the pitcher and offered it to me.

"No danger there." I held my hand over my glass to indicate I didn't want any more tea. "My ticket to heaven was probably torn up a long time ago."

"I doubt that, Missy." V.A. gently tapped the table with her fingers, her voice softening.

"Thanks for that." My eyes rested on hers. V.A. was a rock made of common sense and a firm attitude. I was going to miss her.

Standing on the porch to say our good-byes, I finally asked the question that had been bugging me ever since I first read her sign out front. "V.A.?"

"Yeah?" She pressed her fists into her sides as she surveyed her yard.

"Would you mind telling me what the V.A. stands for?"

With a grin in her eyes, she looked over at me. "You're going to have to wait for the next visit for the answer to that one."

"But?" I raised my shoulders and turned my palms up.

"You'll be back," she said, with a confident tone.

She was wrong about that one. I reached my hand out. "Thanks again for sharing your time and your bathroom with me. I wish you and your family well."

"My pleasure, Missy." She squeezed mine and patted the back of it. "Safe travels."

As I made my way out to the street, she hollered after me, "I'll call you the next time I need an assistant for a calf pulling!"

Raising my hand in good-bye, I smiled and called back, "You do that!"

With a lot of time to kill before I estimated Cal would knock off for the day, I decided to have a late lunch at Dusty's. Taking a seat at the counter, I was the only diner in the restaurant other than a pair of ranchers in a corner booth talking over coffee. Noticing Dusty's torso in the kitchen and not seeing Dori anywhere, I spoke up. "Hey, Dusty."

Responding, he bent down and grinned like we were old friends. "Hey there. What can I get ya?"

"Okay, this may qualify as an obsession, but is it possible to get an order of the buffalo Bolognese? It's my last chance to have it. I'm leaving tomorrow."

"You just have exceptional taste, Missy." He chuckled and wiped his hands on his apron. "It's usually a dinner item, but if you don't mind waiting a little extra time, I can put some together for you."

"I don't want to be any trouble."

"Happy to do it."

"Thanks. Dori not around?" I asked, before he disappeared back into the kitchen.

"No. But, she and Luke will be here soon to get ready for the dinner shift. I'll be out in a minute with your water."

I took my time eating, lingering over the pie and ice cream that Dusty had rustled up while I waited for Dori. I was definitely not in any danger of losing weight during my confinement in Harmony.

When Dori and Luke walked through the door, Luke headed to the kitchen and she came right over to me.

Taking the stool next to mine, she said, her voice somber, "So, Gloria and Joannie; Crane found them."

"Yeah, I'm so sorry."

"He said you and Noah were out there last night."

"Yeah. *You* didn't go out there did you?"

"No. We didn't know anything until this morning. By the time I heard, the bodies were already moved to the morgue in St. George."

"That's just as well."

"A part of me was expecting it, and another part still can't believe there are people who are that ..." Dori rubbed her fingers across her forehead.

"Evil," I filled in.

"Yeah. Evil."

"The part I can't understand is how Helen, Agnes, the nephews, and the rest could even look at each other without feeling shame or guilt or remorse. They make no effort to stop Samuel from doing it again. It's crazy." I released my hand from my coffee cup, realizing I had been gripping it so tight it could break.

"No. *They're* crazy! Certifiable. Really. That's what brainwashing does to you."

"You helped put an end to it, *for them*, at least. You should feel very proud of the work you and the others have done." I set my hand on top of Dori's, which was resting on the counter. "Now, you have an opportunity to help the younger ones. There's a spark in Angela. You can see it. She still has a chance at a normal life."

"*They* have an opportunity to help the younger ones. *I'm leaving.* I'm through." Dori breathed in then let out a deep sigh.

"That's it, huh?"

"Yeah. Just as soon as Luke and I can pack up, we're on our way. I want to get him into a school in L.A. very soon. I'm sure the new term is starting."

"For you too, right?"

"Yeah." She flipped her hair back over her shoulders. "If I can. It may be too late for this semester, but that gives me more time to put money away. Thanks for putting me on to Harry, by the way. He's been a big help already. It sounds like he's even willing to help us find a place to live."

"That's Harry."

"Why'd you leave the guy, anyway?"

"The whole uncomfortable with being comfortable thing went for him too. Nuts, right? Giving up a great guy." Picking up my fork, I pressed the tines down on the crumbs left on the pie plate.

"Hey, it was best for both of you that you left if you doubted your commitment to him. It would have been totally unfair to him to be living with someone who was just settling. He deserves to be with a woman who thinks he's the greatest thing in the world."

"Ouch." I grimaced. "That sure makes me sound shallow."

"No. You knew you had to move on. That's the most important thing. Settling is never good for anyone. And that goes for work too, by the way. As soon as you can get away from editing, do it!" She stared me down.

"And you with waitressing, right!"

"Right!" She smiled a rare smile that was a glimpse into a life for Dori that might contain far more moments of joy than she had ever known.

As Luke passed by the counter, his hands full of utensils, I said, "Hey, can you stop for a minute?"

Looking down at his hands, he seemed hesitant. "I need to set the tables."

"That's okay, Lucas, you can finish in a minute," Dori intervened. "Sydney wants to talk to you."

"I just wanted to tell you I'm leaving tomorrow to continue my trip in the motorhome."

"Oh. Okay." He focused on the utensils. "You are going all the way across the country, right?"

"Yes. All the way to New York."

"I'd like postcards." He raised his eyes and fixed them on a point over my shoulder.

"Okay, I'd be happy to send you postcards, once Dori lets me know your address in L.A."

"Good. Yes, we are going to L.A. It is going to be good, right Dori?" He shifted his gaze in her direction.

"Yes, it's going to be *very* good."

"And then, I am going to Alaska. In a motorhome."

"To see the Aurora Borealis," I added, smiling at him.

"Yes, to see the Aurora Borealis." He looked off in the distance, contemplating a dancing night sky, I supposed.

"And then, it will be your turn to send postcards to *me.*"

"Yes. I will send postcards to you."

"I look forward to it." I was tempted to reach out and touch his arm, but smiled again instead.

"Well, I best get to work." Dori popped up.

"Then, I guess this is good-bye." I slid off my stool, facing her. Closing the gap between us, I wrapped my arms around her and embraced her tightly. She didn't resist, returning my hug.

When I stepped out of the embrace, I said, "You're a power for good, Dori Hunt. It's been a privilege to get to know you. A bright spot in my week in Harmony."

"It's been great to meet you too." She adjusted her earring. "This isn't good-bye though, right?" Her tone vacillated from a statement to a question, and in that moment, I recognized a vulnerability that sought reassurance that this was the beginning, not the end, of a relationship.

"No, it isn't. I'll be checking up on you to see how you're enjoying the L.A. traffic." I smiled.

"So, off we go, then. To new lives." She reached for my hand and pressed hers into it.

"To new lives." I cupped my free hand over our joined ones.

CHAPTER TWENTY-ONE

True to his word, Cal had the motorhome finished just before noon on Tuesday. Was there ever any doubt?

Pulling it through his gate for me, he turned off the ignition and hopped out. "She's purrin' like a kitten," he said as I walked over to him. "Good as new."

With pink and green graffiti bleeding through Lucas' splotchy paint job, referring to Uncle George's RV as new was a tad generous, but so long as it ran, whatever Cal wanted to think was fine by me.

"Thank you, again. I appreciate your letting me stay in your yard all week." I took a last look around, thinking no one would ever believe this.

"No skin off me." Cal jutted out his hand when I glanced back at him.

I grabbed it, grease, or no grease, and held on while he gave mine a good shake. "Sure you don't want any pronghorn, now?" He finally let go. "I got some that makes a might tasty stew."

"No, I'm good. Thanks, though." I pulled my purse from my shoulder and grabbed for the door handle.

"You mind you don't get lost now." Cal shut the door for me once I was tucked into the cab.

"I'll try not to."

"And next time you're here, I'll see that dog of yours gets a good run with mine, maybe even do a little coon huntin'."

Now, there was an offer I didn't get every day. "I'm not going to be back, Cal," I said, then felt bad for being so blunt when he looked puzzled by my response.

"Well, that is, I don't plan to be."

"Never know about them plans." He pulled his baseball cap off and wiped his forehead with his sleeve.

Watching him, I had to admit there was a gentleman of a different sort, but nonetheless a gentleman, under all that stubble and grease. "Hey, thanks too for coming to my rescue that night with the Bailey boys. I hate to think what might have happened if you hadn't been there."

"It wasn't nothin'." He put his cap back on.

"Yes, it *was something*, Cal. You're a brave guy."

Unable to come up with something to say for once, he shifted from one leg to the next.

"Well again, thanks." I turned the key in the ignition.

In response, he tugged on the brim of his cap, then turned and whistled for his dogs.

Making my way down Main Street for the last time, I took a long look at the buildings, filled with the same disbelief as when I first laid eyes on Harmony, that places like this still exist. Just past V.A.'s house, I noticed a familiar truck heading my direction. I pulled over when I saw it stop on the opposite side of the street.

As Noah crossed over to me, his hat, and his gait now so familiar, I felt that same schoolgirl rush as when Johnny Stewart walked passed me in the hall at Chrysler Elementary. It made me want to bash my head on the steering wheel. But, I refrained.

"Thought you were going to get away without saying good-bye?" he said, without a smile, after I rolled down my window.

"I thought we'd said our good-byes."

"Did you?"

"Well yeah, you know, last night."

"You want to step on out here."

"Well, I ..."

"It's not a question." His eyes locked on mine, as he opened the door.

When I hopped down out of the RV, he took his hat off, set it on the driver's seat, and shut the door.

Stepping in front of me, he ran his arms around my back, pressed his body into mine, bent his head and kissed me, without any soft prelude. No, this was one long, hard, deep kiss that shot a bolt of heat from my head to my toes.

Holy shit!

When he finally pulled back, his face was still inches away. With his breath on my skin, his eyes penetrated mine for a long moment, he kissed me again, running his hands down the length of my spine and pulling me so tight to him I felt every button, zipper, muscle, and bone.

Then he let go, just like that; opened the motorhome door, grabbed his hat from the cab, and started back across the street.

"That's not fair!" I yelled after him, when I recovered enough to catch my breath.

Never turning around, he combed his fingers through his hair, waved his hat, and set it on his head.

"It *wasn't* fair," I said to Alice who was curled up on the passenger seat.

Listening to the sound of Noah's engine fading in the distance, as I started my own I looked over my shoulder at Mr. Bumbles, who was plopped on his side right behind us.

"Well, kids, your human may be making the biggest mistake of her life–or not–but I guess we'll soon find out."

Author's Note

The title for *Finding Harmony* came to me very early in the writing process. It felt perfect from the start, because not only was *Harmony* a factor in Sydney's quest, it was also a name well suited to the locale of my fictitious town in Southern Utah–an area settled by Mormon pioneers, miners, farmers, ranchers, and the occasional outlaw.

I was more right than I realized at the time.

Due to other obligations, it took me almost three years to complete *Finding Harmony*, and it wasn't until over two years into the process that I discovered there was a *New* Harmony, Utah. In looking into its history, I discovered that New Harmony was settled by families forced to evacuate from Fort Harmony, after most of its adobe walls were washed away by the Great Flood of 1862. I also read that the total population was about 190 in the 2000 census. Contemplating that, I decided there would be little basis for comparison between the real New Harmony and the Harmony of my imagination.

With the release of the second edition of *Finding Harmony*, I decided to update my website and include information about issues such as polygamy and human trafficking. While searching the Internet to become current with the latest news on polygamists, I discovered a non-profit group that works with refugees of polygamy that was new to me. When I clicked on their contact information, I had to look twice, for they are located–yes, you guessed it–in New Harmony, Utah.

Of course, I called.

The woman I talked with, who left polygamy at the age of fifty, graciously shared some of her own story and much about the ongoing struggle of the victims of polygamy. She also told me that her town has grown quite a bit since 2000, and there is now a polygamist group living nearby. I shared my story about the connection between my fictional town and hers, and told her I would include information about her organization on my website. You will find it by going to: susanhartsnyder.com.

Gotta love that serendipity!

Sydney's next escapade—in the Big Apple—places her in the path of a criminal organization with a long and dangerous reach. How's she going to extract herself from this latest mess? Will Harmony remain a fading image in her rearview mirror? Find out in *Caught in Traffic*, a delicious blend of mystery and suspense, moxie, and humor.